BOUNTY
HUNTRESS

BOUNTY HUNTRESS

SLEEPY HOLLOW HUNTER: BOOK ONE

Sheri Queen

Cover design by X-Potion Designs

Editing by Carrie Gessner

ISBN-10: 0692803378
ISBN-13: 978-0692803370

For Stuart

~Angels Walk Among Us~

Acknowledgments

There are many people to thank for this story coming to fruition. My heartfelt gratitude goes out to all of them, especially my family:

Mom & Dad
Don
Tim, Colleen, Mike, Cavan, Erin, David
Jan
Stuart

A special thank-you to my writing family at Seton Hill University's Writing Popular Fiction program. They gave graciously of their time and knowledge to guide me through this endeavor. In particular, thank you to Annika for reading through the draft; Amy, Carrie G., and Carrie M. for all the countless questions they answered for me. You guys rock!

Thank you for purchasing this book.

If you enjoyed the story, please consider leaving a review where you purchased it or on your blog or Goodreads. Reviews directly impact visibility to new readers, so every review is greatly appreciated. Thank you!

Bounty Huntress is the introduction to the Sleepy Hollow Hunter series. For more information on Sheri and the Sleepy Hollow Hunter series, visit sheriqueen.com.

Bounty Huntress is a Hotel Paranormal story.

The Hotel Paranormal is the place for supernatural beings looking to get away from it all. Beings like werewolves, vampires, elves, sprites, djinn and more check in from all over the world for business and for pleasure — and sometimes for both.
www.thehotelparanormal.com

CHAPTER ONE
Mutther's

Whoever said "happiness is an inside job" sure as hell didn't know me. I preferred happiness that came from external sources, like bringing criminals to justice. Not that I cared for the justice part, but I sure derived a sense of satisfaction from the paycheck. Bounty hunters had a reputation for being self-serving, and I was no different than the rest. It was all about the money — not making friends — and this job would buy me *a lot* of happiness.

I repeated it several times, because fun was not something I was having at the moment. Pushing a Harley 1200 for half a mile on an old country road — hitting potholes in the middle of the night — to get the drop on some werewolves had seemed like a good idea at one point, but I was having second thoughts as sweat beaded across my forehead. I tucked Miss Kitty into the shelter of a side alley and threw the tarp I'd brought over the sleek motorcycle. It'd either be here when I returned — *if* I returned — or it wouldn't. I gave my ride a final pat and slipped into the nighttime shadows near the alley entrance, staying downwind and praying the whiskey I'd splashed over myself would mask my scent. A woman — and worse, a Lykoi — didn't just walk into a place frequented by Dominant bikers. It was especially true in a small town where everyone knew one another.

There were protocols to follow and introductions to be made before approaching a one-percenter, and I doubted anyone would step forward to sponsor someone like me. I was half wolf and had been raised by a prominent pack in the area just outside the town of Sleepy Hollow, New York. I existed on the fringes of my pack, shunned for being part werecat. Most of the time I didn't mind going solo. It was how I lived. It also meant I wouldn't have to share the bounty reward that would give me the freedom I sought. Once I lured my target from the Hotel Paranormal and turned him over to my client, I'd have everything I'd ever wanted — a one-way ticket away from pack prejudices and a new life as a financially secure recluse. I flicked my tongue along my lips, tasting the freedom this deal would bring.

Half a block stood between me and my future happiness, but it might as well have been a mile for all the good it would do me. From the alley to the bar there was no cover, no shadows to absorb my presence. I'd scoured the surrounding area for another entry point to no avail. Barred windows and a padlocked backdoor thwarted me. I had one shot at getting inside before anyone could stop me, and that meant waiting until the barkeep kicked the last of his patrons out at closing time. While they were busy getting on their bikes, I'd make a mad dash to the front door. I was grateful the street was deserted at this hour, but it was almost too quiet. One stupid move on my part could mean disaster.

I calculated the distance from where I stood, hidden in the alley, to the bar's entrance and figured I'd probably be fast enough to make it as long as the wolves were so drunk they wouldn't notice me until it was too late. It was a long shot, but the only one I had. Wolves were quick, even inebriated ones. Their metabolism burned off alcohol within minutes of downing it, which meant my window of opportunity was about the size of a mouse hole. In my Lykoi state I was faster than a wolf—I'd honed that particular skill long ago with all the times I'd been chased—but I couldn't go Lykoi. Paws didn't lend themselves to turning doorknobs, so I'd have to do this the hard way. Nothing new there.

I leaned against the brick wall and let the cool autumn air soothe my restless body. My calf muscles twitched, and my stomach rumbled. It was tempting to give in to the urge to transform and run through the woods I'd passed on the way into town. Maybe even hunt a bit of rabbit. I let out a slow breath and resisted my primal desires.

I counted four bikes outside the bar. Mutther's might be a neutral, no-colors establishment, but I still had to get past the owners of those bikes. Four big-ass obstacles between me and the portal to the Hotel Paranormal. I knew portals existed in most major cities—definitely in Manhattan—but, of course, my only way into the hotel would be through a wolf biker bar. My luck ranged from bad to stinking bad. I was long overdue for a bit of good luck, but I didn't look for that to happen tonight. My usual mode of blending into the background to avoid attracting

attention wasn't going to work here. There were no
crowds to lose myself in, and the glaring neon sign
covering three quarters of the bar's facade was a
beacon spreading a swath of red across the sidewalk.
Anyone wishing to enter the bar would be doused in
light. This had to be the hotel's idea of a joke—or a
test.

I pinned my hopes for survival on Mutther's
neutrality. As long as I got in the bar and stayed in,
I'd be safe. I wasn't stupid enough to think the
wolves would make it easy if they saw me. They'd
follow—to hell with whether the bar was closing. I
had to find the portal as soon as I slipped inside, or I
might accidentally-on-purpose get shoved back
outside where it'd be open season for a certain
female bounty hunter. It's a good thing I could
transform on the run.

On my ride north, I had lots of time to think of a
decent plan, but this was the best I could come up
with. I tried to ignore the fact that most of my plans
blew up in my face—sometimes literally. I rubbed at
the patch of hair that was still growing in from one of
my last bounty hunter adventures. I'd had to
improvise by styling a ragged, one-sided cut, which
brought out the white streak in my black hair, but I
liked the new shorter version, so silver lining, make
lemonade when life hands you lemons, whatever. I
did okay then, and I'd make do now, unless I
couldn't get through the inter-dimensional portal.
There was no guarantee the damn thing would open
for me, even with the business card I had stowed in
the back pocket of my jeans. To most people, the little
card with *the Hotel* printed on it wouldn't garner a

passing thought. To those who possessed one, it was the way into the Hotel Paranormal. I did a quick check to be sure it was still there and wondered what it had cost my client to obtain my admittance. It couldn't have been cheap. Money or favors seemed to be the only way to access the exclusive hotel. Yeah, the case had high-risk factors like death or maiming —neither of which I wanted to experience—but I couldn't pass on the reward.

I perked up at the sound of the front door banging open. The red neon beacon flashed alarmingly close as if daring me to make my move. I balanced my weight on the balls of my feet anticipating the exact moment the little mouse hole of opportunity would show itself. I cleared my head of any thoughts of failure. I had this.

But Fate hated me. She truly did. I placed one foot into the red zone, waiting for the club leader to finish struggling into his vest so he'd turn away from my alley and towards his bike, when my mouse hole of an entrance was blocked by a rather large guy. From the heavy flavor of his scent reaching me, it was another wolf. Not one of the bikers. Shit!

I flattened against the wall, hissing my disgruntlement in a slurry of curses, and stared up at the half-moon slowly being consumed by clouds.

"One break. I just need one."

If any greater powers existed, I hoped they were listening, because I didn't stand a chance otherwise. I inched closer to the edge of the building so I could keep an eye on the group gathered in front of the bar.

"Hey, Mutther," slurred the club leader.

"Yeah?" Mutther stepped out from the doorway,

but not far enough to widen the mouse hole.

"You're a good sport, man. Damn good sport."

The leader had gotten into his vest and had managed to find purchase on his seat. The booze buzz must have started fading, and with it, my plan. There was that bad luck again. The other three revved their bikes, waiting for the word to take off, but their leader was too talkative. I ground my teeth at the inane conversation.

The lead biker pointed a finger at Mutther and shouted over the engine noise. "Next time the last drinks are on me, even if you lose again. You don't have much of a poker face. Easy win."

"Sure was," Mutther said, grinning from ear to ear, "and I hate to break it to you, but you lost. The drinks are on your tab."

"What the fuck?"

Deep billows of laughter filled the street. I would have laughed too, if my current situation weren't so bleak. Instead, I recalculated my chances of making it past the bar owner. Slim to none. Not good odds, but I never paid attention to odds.

"Later, Nick." Mutther waved the bikers off and started back inside.

Nick huffed a couple of times as if he had more to say on the matter, but the words stuck in his throat until he gave up on the effort and kick-started his bike. It roared to life and the four men took off down the street, spraying a fine trail of grit behind them. I didn't wait to see if they'd glance back my way. I ran for the door that was almost shut, not caring about being in the red zone. Stealth didn't matter anymore. Mutther placed his hand on the edge of the door right when I blasted through the entryway. My momentum hurtled me forward, straight into him, knocking him backward. If I hadn't built up speed on my dash, and if he hadn't been caught by surprise, I never would have been able to unbalance him. He was big, strong, and as solid as a mountain. He stared down at me, eyes wide and mouth slightly open, but within a nanosecond he had a tight hold on my wrist.

"Hey," I said, attempting to catch my breath. I didn't try to twist away from his grip, because while my uncle often said I was a glutton for punishment, it wasn't true. I didn't like pain any more than the next sane person and I'd already gotten hurt when I banged into Mutther. I was pretty certain I'd have a few bruises by morning. Mutther continued to stare. I didn't know quite what to say, so I laid it out for him. "Sorry about intruding, but I have to get through the Hotel Paranormal portal as soon as possible." I managed to pull the business card from my pocket with my other hand. My knuckles stung. I'd scraped them when I catapulted through the entrance, but didn't recall exactly how — probably grazed myself on the door plate, which was a typical move for me.

While Mutther appeared to be mulling over his response, I took a moment to get a better look at him. He had an earthy quality about him and not just because he reminded me of a rugged mountain. He didn't seem older than maybe his late thirties, but it was like he belonged to an older time, when nature held reign over men. This was a guy who in another era would have been a worthy king. He noticed me watching, raised an eyebrow, but said nothing, still holding my wrist. I held the card out to him, keeping my bloodied fist from contaminating my ticket into the hotel.

He kicked the door shut and released me to take the card in a blur of motion. If he meant to intimidate me, he had much to learn. I'd grown up with a pack of wolves who took pleasure in taunting me. I knew how to keep my feelings inside — well, most of them. Anger *did* tend to get away from me. I held my ground, never flinching at his movement. At least he hadn't tossed me outside, but the distant rumble of the bikers didn't mean I'd be safe if Mutther changed his mind, so I had to play this right. Although he didn't belong to the gang that had just left, his wolf howl would alert them and they'd be back in a flash, sober — not good for me.

Mutther, however, didn't raise the alarm, and I relaxed a fraction, keeping my mouth shut, which was not an easy task for me. I bit the inside of my lip hard enough to draw blood.

"You sure the hotel will let you in?"

The familiar heat of anger crept up my neck. I wasn't sure about getting into the hotel, and he could see it on my face. I had no idea if the hotel would let half-breeds like me pass the threshold, but my employer hadn't seemed to think it a problem, so why should Mutther? "I have a valid reservation."

He laughed and walked towards the bar. I followed him — fists firmly at my sides — taking in my surroundings. It was a standard bar — dark wood paneling, flat screen centrally located for easy viewing, several smaller screens hung along the back of the bar tuned to different sports channels, round tables that seated four spread haphazardly around the room as if they were constantly being shoved out of place and Mutther had stopped trying to arrange them. A pool table sat in a far corner and a well-used dart board hung on the wall a short distance from a cue rack. Despite its disorderly appearance, the place was spotless. Mutther cared about his establishment. He snagged remotes and turned everything off.

"Newbies," he said.

I had no idea what he meant, but the tone irked me. I might be in my late twenties, but I wasn't a young upstart. I was a seasoned bounty hunter and I was about to remind him of it when he moved off to clear away the last of the drinks.

He grabbed a cleaning rag and rubbed the mahogany bar top until my reflection stared back at me, revealing the frustration and resentment I felt boiling just beneath my skin.

"Reservations don't mean shit. Your admittance card can be wiped clean," he continued. "The *hotel* decides who gets in."

He emphasized hotel as if the place had a mind of its own. I sat on a stool directly in front of Mutther and ignored my reflection. "Suppose you tell me how you know all this. I have it on good authority that I shouldn't have any problems with my reservation." It was a white lie, and I had an inkling he knew it. "The problem I have is the entry point." I swept my arm in an arc to encompass the bar. "Not exactly the most convenient location for a portal, if you're someone like me."

Mutther actually frowned at that. I hid my surprise but wished I knew what he was thinking for him to have such a reaction. I'd expected him to be judgmental or at the least indifferent. Both reactions I'd grown accustomed to when meeting people for the first time. My kind tended to elicit such responses.

"I suppose you have a point."

He carefully folded the rag and stowed it behind the counter. He poured two shots of whiskey and handed me one, meeting my gaze. "What I meant was the hotel is a safe harbor. It won't allow harm to come to its guests." He eyed me a long moment over the brim of his glass before downing his drink.

"My intentions are harmless." I said it with conviction, but a tiny part of me buried in the recesses of my conscience called me a liar. I didn't have malevolent motives, but my actions could hardly be called harmless. I was after Alexander Holden, who was accused of murdering his betrothed. His future, and possibly his life, was at stake. I knew it, but did the hotel?

"Then I guess it's time you used the bathroom." He pointed down the dimly lit hall to a nondescript wooden door.

"Excuse me?"

A wry smile spread across Mutther's face. "It's the only bathroom I have, and it happens to double as the portal, but only to those able to see it."

The realization of his words hit me hard. My pulse quickened as doubt crept up my throat, making my response barely more than a whisper. "So I might not see it?"

Mutther nodded.

"Fantastic." I hopped off the stool and headed

down the hall. Mutther hadn't budged, but I could feel his gaze on my back. I hesitated for the briefest moment with one hand against the wooden surface and my other on the handle. I cast a look back at Mutther. "Wish me luck."

"Luck."

He hadn't said 'good luck,' just 'luck,' but I'd take it just the same.

I turned the knob and opened the door a few inches. "Wait," Mutther said, catching up with me. He handed me the business card I'd given him. "You'll need this to enter the hotel. The portal is simply the first step."

As soon as I took it, light emanated from the partially open door. I prayed it was a good omen.

I had no idea how many steps I'd climb to reach my destination or if the steps he mentioned were true steps, but he knew more than I did. "By the way, I'm Janda. Thanks for your help."

"The name's Matthias. And you're welcome."

I cocked my head, as if that would clear everything up. "If your name isn't Mutther, then why did the bikers call you that? And why does your neon sign say it? Isn't this your bar?" My curiosity made my usual tactlessness worse. I hurried to retract the questions before I annoyed him too much. "Never mind. It doesn't matter. Thanks for letting me use the . . . bathroom." I gave him a smile I hoped would make up for any blundering on my part.

He grinned. "It's cool. Yes, this is my bar. No, my name isn't Mutther. It's a nickname that kind of stuck."

"Oh. I see." I didn't really but refused to keep

putting my foot in my mouth. I felt warmth coming from the light seeping through and wanted nothing more than to continue onward.

Matthias moved close enough for me to feel his breath on my shoulders, then my neck. It was the slow stalking of a predator and it put my senses on high alert. I applied more pressure against the door. It creaked open.

"Thanks again," I said.

"Matthias Utther at your service." He did a mock bow and stepped back, giving me free access to the portal.

I stepped forward, paused as the knowledge of what he said sunk in, and spun back to him. "Ah. I get it. First initial and last name." I chuckled.

"Fast learner," he said. "You'll need it where you're going."

My smile faded.

"Just watch your back. That's all I'm saying."

"Sure thing," I said, dreading pushing the door all the way open. Fear finally rose to the surface. Why did he have to go and say that? I understood why he'd gone all predator on me. I needed to be on my guard and he'd just played on my survival instincts to get me ready for what would come.

Before I could go any farther, Mutther grabbed me for the second time that night, held my arm, forced me to slow down and not rush through the portal the way I'd rushed through his front door.

"I'm serious about being careful. Unless the hotel allows you to use a different portal on your return, you'll have to come back through here. Your best bet is to aim for when the bar is closed, otherwise you could end up smack in the middle of a full house. That wouldn't be in your best interest."

I swallowed some of my fear. "No, it wouldn't."

His hold on me tightened. "The hotel can play tricks on you, taunt you, goad you into doing things, but it always does what it thinks is best for its guests. It also wouldn't hesitate to throw you out to the wolves — if it felt you deserved it — get my drift."

Unfortunately, I did. "Thanks for the warning."

He released me and I crossed over the threshold.

CHAPTER TWO
Hotel Paranormal

If dying was like this, I'd take it. I had passed through the all-encompassing light of Mutther's bathroom and ended up standing next to a statue of Athena in front of a massive stone mansion—the grandest building I'd ever seen. The business card felt warm in my pocket where I'd stowed it just before going through the portal. It was as if it knew it was home and was urging me to stop gawking, so it could be delivered into the hands of its creator. I took one step and stopped. The place was truly magnificent, and I wasn't.

Marble pillars held up a massive portico where guests could enter the hotel protected from the elements, although I had the impression that the weather would never be an issue. It was still nighttime. The warm air held the scent of flowers that hovered all around me—sweet, spicy, woodsy—enticing me to breathe deeply, relax, give over to its magic. I didn't know where I was or even when. Perhaps that's what Mutther had tried to warn me about. Here in this dimension anything was possible.

Two women in 1930s gowns with plunging necklines and beaded fabric—bedecked with jewels the size of oysters—were accompanied by equally elegant gentlemen. The way they glided up to the entrance was a giant cue they weren't human. Vamps most likely. I hadn't seen them until they were just there, emerging from nothingness, which made me wonder if you could only detect your own portal. They drifted between the front pillars and were met by a valet who pulled on the long brass handle to open the door for them. From my vantage point I glimpsed a large fountain in the lobby. The flow of water greeted me in a whispered voice of welcome, drawing me closer.

I couldn't help but move towards the hotel. Besides, my alternative was to go back to the bar, which was no choice at all. Even though I was a creature of the streets—with no place in this high society setting—I had to stay. Maybe this was the hotel teasing me and letting me get within reach of my target before shutting me out. My riding gear and ragged haircut were the least of my issues. I rubbed my boots together to dislodge crusted dirt. It didn't help. I sighed, tugged at my jacket, and strode up to the entrance. The door didn't open at my approach. I hesitated, unsure of what to do.

The valet, whose gold name tag proclaimed him to be David, stood no more than three feet tall—barely above my waist. He gave me a skeptical look, but in an instant donned his mask of professionalism. Not that I normally gave a damn what anyone thought about how I dressed. Mine was a practical wardrobe. Easy on, easy off, for shifting on the run. I valued practicality and at the moment that meant I had to at least pretend to fit in.

"Luggage, Miss?"

Luggage? I had the clothes on my back and a hefty advance on my pay. That was it. If the hotel had a boutique, perhaps I'd be able to find the essentials I'd need for a short stay—very short one, since my daily expense advance wouldn't go far. The place unsettled me more than I'd admit.

"I don't have any. It's a brief visit."

"Well, then," David said, opening the door. "Have a most pleasant evening."

His expertly groomed mustache twitched above his expertly groomed beard, and he stood with his back ramrod straight in his expertly pressed uniform. I felt slovenly in comparison. I stifled a sigh. So much for not caring what others thought of me. Not even through the front door, and old feelings of inadequacy surfaced—and at the hands of a person who could be an evening snack, he was so small. This was not going to be like my usual contracts.

"Thanks," I said, smiling. It was one of my better features and when properly employed aided me in disarming my acquaintances. I didn't use it often, but I figured I'd need to use it a lot more at a place like this one. Steps, Mutther had said. There were many steps to reach my goal. Now I understood steps came in various shapes and sizes, and it would require me to be astute enough to recognize them.

David said evening, which implied the night was just getting started, but I'd crossed through the portal at the predawn hour. Time was definitely different here. There'd be no way for me to schedule my departure to coincide with Mutther's bar being closed. As usual, nothing was easy.

I stepped into the vast lobby with its blood-red carpet that had tiny black flowers that reminded me of ants. But it was the fountain that commanded the room. It was huge. Paranormal creatures had been carved meticulously into the stone. Upon closer examination it appeared to have every creature imaginable. Some I didn't recognize at all. I walked around its base, but nowhere did I see a creature like me.

"This way, Miss." David had come up behind me and waited to take me to the check-in desk. I tagged along after him, impressed by his stealth. I have pretty damn good hearing, and I never heard him approach. Perhaps the fountain had other functions besides adornment.

Standing behind a striking walnut reception desk was one of the tallest men I'd ever seen. I pegged him at about seven and a half feet. His skin was as dark as the wood his hands rested on and his black suit was cut in a classic, timeless style. Even his bald head added to his distinguished appearance. He smiled at me, not in the condescending way I was used to, but with warm cordialness that immediately put me at ease. I couldn't help but like him. He wasn't human, but I didn't know exactly what he was, only that something about him made me physically calmer. I'd known of predators that could do that right before they killed you. Lulled into complacency the victim never sees it coming. Not this guy. I got the impression his smile was genuine. I sniffed the air as inconspicuously as possible. A mild scent like summer rain rolling off flower petals greeted me. It came from him.

"Hi, I'm Janda Gray. Checking in for a few days." I laid the business card, now bent from handling it so much, in front of him. He never glanced at it, just kept his focus on me.

"My name is Max. Your room is ready for you, Miss Gray." His smile reached his dark brown eyes in an enticing way.

"Thank you. Um, that's very efficient." I took the key he proffered, avoiding his gaze. Max seemed like a nice guy, but there was an *otherness* about him that unsettled me even with the calm he exuded. Instead, I scrutinized the object I held in my palm. The key was a rectangular brass tab with a red rectangular gem in the center. I flipped it over thinking my room number would be inscribed on the back. Nada. Nothing at all to indicate which door it fit—and no magnetic strip.

Max must have guessed what I was thinking, or he really did know what I was thinking, because his smile broadened.

"We have no need for room numbers here. David can explain as he takes your belongings upstairs."

"I don't have any luggage."

"No matter. The Hotel will provide for your needs." His eyes twinkled knowingly. "I work the night shift," he said, "so if there's anything you need, please don't hesitate to call. Your room phone will automatically connect you to the front desk. Please enjoy your stay." He gave me a short nod and motioned for David to come forward.

"Thanks." I gave Max the once-over and wondered just what kind of hotel I'd entered.

"If you please," David said, holding his hand out

in the direction of the lobby.

We wound around the fountain, and I couldn't help but be drawn to it by the lulling splash of water flowing over the tiers to land in the circular basin. A grand staircase rose high above us to the right of the lobby, but David took me to an elevator rather than the stairs. Both had been hewn from mahogany and polished to a rich tone of perfection that enhanced the grandeur of the architecture.

At his approach the elevator doors spread apart in expectation. David stood aside for me to enter first. The inside was also paneled in rich mahogany with mirrors embedded in the walls. The floor selector had one button, although I was sure just from the view I had of it outside that the hotel had more than two floors. David pressed it. The doors closed. I still had no idea where he was taking me.

"Sorry, but I don't recall Max saying which room I'll be staying in and on which floor. I'm sure you won't be able to be my constant guide, so I'd appreciate a brief explanation of the hotel's layout."

The elevator continued to rise with such smoothness it was impossible to detect how many floors we'd risen. I was beginning to feel uncomfortable. I had to get my bearings if I was to go exploring on my own.

David took a deep breath. "I'll begin at the beginning." He paused expectantly.

"Please do," I replied.

He had my full attention, which must have been his intent. David liked an avid audience for a tale he seemed to have memorized, or had lived with for so long that it was ingrained in him, and was eagerly about to impart on fresh ears such as mine.

"The Hotel Paranormal is steeped in history so ancient few have any clue as to when its foundation was first laid. I for one am not privy to that information, so don't bother asking such things." He spoke matter-of-factly in a response he used to cut through the typical tourist inquiries.

I kept my mouth shut and my gaze on him. He stood as tall as his stature would allow and squared his shoulders.

"The Hotel, as we like to call it, has a host of secrets locked within its walls—some you will come to understand and many more you won't. Your room and the floor it's located on are of no consequence to the Hotel. They exist. That's all you need concern yourself with."

"And I'll know my way around, how?"

He smiled at me as if about to instruct a small child of the wonders of the world. It was an effort to control my annoyance that was escalating the longer I waited for him to say something, anything, that would give me autonomy in this place.

A soft ping and the doors opened. The hall split off to either side of the elevator. The floor was covered in lush carpet as blue as the sky on a clear day and the walls had been painted silver gray, the color of a coming storm. There weren't as many rooms as I had expected, only three in each direction. Mahogany wood seemed to be a theme in the hotel, with its doors and framework polished to a satin finish. Not a smudge or mark to be found. Immaculate. Pristine. Intimidating. I was *so* out of my element.

Two marble goddesses stood sentinel in each direction—Aphrodite and Athena.

Athena's head swiveled to face me, and she raised her right arm, pointing down the hall. I stepped back and almost knocked David over.

He chortled, regained his balance, and led me onward. "They're not alive, but it does take some getting used to when they decide to move."

"You knew that would happen." I wasn't amused.

He shrugged. "Of course, but if I'd warned you it would have been no less shocking, so I prefer to let guests discover the Hotel's idiosyncrasies on their own."

"Thanks. Next time a heads-up would be nice."

"As you wish."

We walked past the statues, and Athena lowered her arm.

"The statues will point the way you need to go. Sometimes, though, they have a sense of humor and will send you in a direction you hadn't expected."

I stopped.

"Oh, don't fret. They never put you in harm's way. The Hotel has strict policies governing such things." He kept going. I followed because what else could I do? We strode past the first two doors.

"Feel anything yet?" he asked.

"Excuse me?"

"The key. How does it feel?"

I hadn't been paying attention, but now that I was, it felt warm. The center stone grew brighter the closer we got to the last door in the corridor. I stared in wonderment. "Warm. It definitely feels warm."

"Good. Then we're heading in the right direction.

Not that I'd ever argue with Athena. She can get a bit testy if you question her judgment."

I nodded. "I can relate."

David chuckled.

I was having trouble absorbing what he'd disclosed — the statues had a mind of their own and the Hotel itself was somehow a sentient being. I'd picked up on how it was referred to as the Hotel, as if that was its name, and found myself doing the same thing. This was way beyond my ability to wrap my brain around, and I'd seen some weird shit in my life.

I realized David had been speaking, and I hastened to catch what he was saying.

"When you get into the elevator, you must be very clear as to your intentions of where you are going. Otherwise, you could confuse it, and who knows where it would take you?" He drew level to my door and appeared to be in no hurry to explain how I was to use my key. He was delighted to give me the Hotel's highlights and kept rambling, extolling its virtues, which I admit were numerous as far as I had seen.

"One level has a fantastic spa," he said. "I highly recommend it. We offer the usual treatments and some more exotic ones to accommodate our diverse guests. The mud bath is quite sensual and a great introduction to the amenities. Then there's the level with the gym. I don't go there much, except to assist a guest who may have wandered off and gotten lost. Like I said, the statues can have a sense of humor."

"I see." What I saw were delays that would make it hard to get my job done on time.

"Ah, but the pool is something you should

partake in while you're here. It's also on its own floor. Huge Turkish-style bath. Unforgettable experience. And of course, it's open all the time. Once you start making your way around, you'll understand that many of our guests have nocturnal inclinations, and we aim to please, no matter what your desires." David took the key from me and held it against the door handle. The gem lit up, then a snap of a lock opening, and we were granted entrance to my room.

I was still hung up on his last words to properly notice my surroundings. There was meaning behind what he'd said that made me wonder what the Hotel knew about my visit. I'd probably be kicked out before morning.

"Your room, Miss Gray."

"Holy crap!"

"Not crap and I assure you not holy." David's voice was smooth and even. He wasn't kidding.

I sobered in an instant. Nothing about this space was crap, although the holy part could be debated. The suite was so ostentatious it was like being in a dream. What lay before me was nothing short of regal, and in my view that made it practically holy. Heavy velvet curtains, as red as garnet, fell in waves across a wide window. The bed was something to behold—a four-poster, ornately carved, so high off the floor I'd need a step stool, and loaded with pillows I could sink into and sleep on for the next century. I *so* wanted to climb into that bed.

"This is divine. No question about it." I ran my fingers along the satin duvet. I'd never seen anything this lovely in my entire life. And yet there were people who took all this for granted. Shame on them.

"I'm glad you approve," David said. He moved into an adjoining room, opened and closed drawers, then returned a moment later. "It appears everything is in order. Your bath has been drawn and the wardrobe is fully stocked with a variety of garments, all of which should be in your size."

"I appreciate the offer of clothing, but I assure you I'm fine with purchasing a few necessities from your boutique."

"We have no need of a boutique. As I mentioned earlier, the Hotel provides for its guests."

I was afraid to ask what happened if I ruined their clothes. I was not the most graceful person on the planet, and my wardrobe was the way it was for a reason. I cringed at the thought of paying for damaged goods.

"I'll leave you to it. Dinner will be served in the main dining room at nine." He pulled a gold pocket watch from his vest, glanced at it and frowned. "Hmm. That only gives you an hour to prepare. I hope that won't inconvenience you too much. If so, I'd be happy to have a tray sent up."

"No. That'll be fine."

"Very well. Do ring if you need anything."

David left as quietly as he'd done when he came up to me at the fountain. He was a man whose nature was to melt into his surroundings, disappearing until he'd suddenly reappear at your elbow, even before you'd asked for his assistance. David was excellent at his job, and I was certain he had other talents the Hotel made ample use of.

I continued my inspection of the room that could

have held my entire apartment. I picked up trinkets and put them carefully back as if I'd been touching museum relics, which some of these might as well have been, before remembering my time limit and heading into the bathroom. I'd stripped down while in the bedroom and grabbed the bathrobe laid out for me. The slippers I left next to the changing area. I preferred to be barefoot whenever possible, and aside from my boots, I didn't feel comfortable in any type of footwear. Maybe it was a result of growing up wolf, or maybe it was the cat in me, that intensified the tactile part of my nature.

Multi-colored bubbles drifted over the water, popping as I sank into the step-down pool that was my bath. Essence of roses burst from pink bubbles, lavender from purple ones, and pine from green. The pine was unexpected, but it suited my mood. I loved the forest and the sense of freedom I got from running among trees in my Lykoi form. I was reluctant to end my bath time, but needs must, so I dried quickly. Dinner would be the first opportunity to observe the Hotel's occupants and hopefully my target.

I reached for my clothes, but they weren't there. Shit. David, or some other stealthy employee, had taken them. I picked up the phone to dial the front desk.

"This is Max. How may I help you?"

His buttery-sweet voice squashed my irritation at my lost clothes, but I wanted them back. "Yes, Max. My clothes seem to have disappeared. I'd like them back. Please." I reminded myself to keep my calm and stay polite.

"Of course, Miss Gray. I understand completely."

Did he now? I doubted it. From the mirth in his voice I assumed he was having a bit of fun with me. I inhaled sharply, closed my eyes, and forced my voice into a state of calm. "I'm so glad you do. Then when can I expect to have them returned? I wanted to go to dinner, but I prefer not to go naked."

Max's laughter boomed over the phone. "I'm so sorry. Truly I am. Please excuse my impertinence. I'll look into this immediately."

"Thank you." I didn't excuse him, because there was no need. I'd developed thick skin over the years. Wolves enjoyed pulling pranks on one another, and especially enjoyed doing it to me. Max's response to my situation was to be expected—annoying, but expected.

I hung up and was pacing naked—deep in thought about how to make contact with my target—when the phone rang.

"Max?"

"It's David, Miss. Sorry for any inconvenience with your clothes, but I should have mentioned that they would be cleaned and returned to you."

"Oh. Well, how long will it take?"

Silence.

"David?"

He cleared his throat. "Yes. I'm not exactly certain. We seem to be having a bit of an issue with the laundry department this evening, but you should have them by morning. My deepest apologies, Miss."

"Morning?" My voice rose. "I can't wait until morning. I need them now. Don't worry about cleaning them. If I have to I can rinse them in my room before bed." I refrained from saying that was how I normally washed my clothes, depending on what I had left after shifting. I tried to be mindful of my clothing when I shifted, but it wasn't easy to keep from tearing them. I had a very limited wardrobe as a result.

"Unfortunately, Miss, I can't give them to you." He paused as if choosing his words. "The, um, laundry department has misplaced them."

"What?" My calm shriveled into a simmering rage. "How do you misplace someone's clothing? How?" I was beginning to stammer. I did that when I lost it.

David spoke in a rush of words I had trouble understanding. His native language was coming through in his speech and whatever it was, I didn't speak it.

"The Hotel does provide for its guests," he said in a reassuring tone, "so you certainly won't be without suitable attire, and I promise you I will personally get to the bottom of this. In the meantime, please help yourself to anything in your wardrobe. I will call you as soon as I have any news. Again, my apologies."

He hung up and I sat on the carpet. Damn. What else could go wrong?

CHAPTER THREE
Unexpected Companion

I pushed the single elevator button with my mind firmly set on the request to go to the dining hall. Then I prayed. I was a big believer in prayers, even though most of mine were never answered. Still, what could it hurt? The doors opened and I faced a ballroom. *Great.* I was about to go back into the elevator, or better yet find the stairs, when the aroma of food reached me. This was the dining room? *Unbelievable.* I stood next to a large potted fern in an attempt to remain inconspicuous for a few minutes. I wanted to get a better look at what I was about to walk into. Several women wore long, sequined gowns and had feather plumes gracing their coiffured hair.

I glanced down at my hemline. *Lovely.* I looked like a hooker.

I'd spent almost half an hour scouring the array of garments provided for something I could wear to dinner. The undergarments hadn't been an issue. I liked silk. It was smooth against my skin and made me feel feminine. However, I didn't wear dresses— had made it a mission in life not to wear them. Dresses took femininity to the extreme for me. So of course that was all the Hotel had to offer. A full range of dresses. Long ones, short ones, beaded and plain ones, most in blacks and reds. I like black and red, just not in dresses. Black was my signature color. A dash of red, like a sleeveless tank top to hide blood stains, was also acceptable. But this?

I'd almost called for room service. Almost. If I didn't have to scope out the dinner guests, I would have shut myself up and waited until my clothes could be found. David, however, had never called, and I was fairly certain I wouldn't hear from him any time soon. I had ended up choosing a simple black dress. It was short, very short, and had a plunging V-neck. A quick twirl in front of the floor-length mirror had me thinking perhaps the Hotel *did* know what it was doing. I wanted to draw Alexander Holden out of his hiding, and if this skimpy number did the trick, I'd revel in wearing it—but that sentiment vanished with my current predicament.

I wanted to hide. What tricks was this blasted Hotel up to this time? How could I go in to dinner dressed like a floozy, when the other women were modestly attired?

"Ah, Mademoiselle. Would you honor me by joining me for dinner?"

A man with paper-thin white skin stood before me, waiting on my response. His veins crisscrossed over his face and neck to give him a blue luminosity that was actually beautiful. He wore a black tuxedo and held a top hat under one arm.

"I'm sorry, but I was just leaving."

"But why? Have you eaten already? Am I too late to request your fine company?"

His crestfallen face was a good act. I wasn't buying it. No one talks like that anymore. I mean no one. My silence should have been enough to convince him not to mess with me, but he didn't leave.

"If you are absolutely certain I can't change your mind, I will be obliged to see you safely to your room."

Right. Now we were getting to the heart of things —the dress—floozy—that's what he assumed. I sighed. "That won't be necessary, thanks. I know my way around." A total lie of course.

"Really? Then I must be sure to stay in your company, because I find it rather difficult to know where I will end up each time I enter the elevator."

I laughed. I couldn't help it. He'd zeroed in on my own concerns not just about the elevator, but the whole establishment.

"The truth is I haven't had dinner and I'm starving. However—" I paused and ran a hand down my waist to the short hem "—I don't appear to be dressed appropriately."

"Posh," he said, taking my elbow and guiding me through the entryway. "Conformity is a misconception. Being true to who you are is real beauty."

"Thank you."

He inclined his head in a slight bow. "You are most welcome, Mademoiselle . . .?"

"Janda."

"I'm Sebastian. Very pleased to make your acquaintance."

I was seated with my cloth napkin spread over

my lap before I had a chance to worry if people were staring at me. Sebastian had talents. He sat across from me and gestured for the waiter, who responded at once by pouring our wine.

"What can I do for you tonight, Sir?" he said.

"My usual please."

The waiter nodded. "Of course. And you, Miss?"

His tone was cordial, and he stood poised to take my order with quiet professionalism. There were no menus. I didn't know what to order. I followed Sebastian's lead.

"I'll have the same."

Sebastian's eyes grew wide and his lips twitched as if he wanted to smile, making me wonder what I'd just done. The waiter didn't miss a beat.

"Very well," he said, glancing at Sebastian, who shrugged. "Your order will be ready momentarily."

I waited until he left before addressing my dinner companion. "What did I just order?"

"Blood pudding," he said. "More blood than pudding. It's a favorite of mine."

"I can handle blood pudding." I was a carnivore for crying out loud. Raw meats were my mainstay. I'd never eaten blood pudding but figured I'd give it a go.

"I believe you can," he said. He took a sip of red wine and seemed content to sit in silence for the time being.

The dinner guests kept a constant stream of conversation going on around us that fell to the background in a steady hum. Sebastian absently fiddled with his knife.

"You're rather quiet, and judging from the table

you picked here in the corner, I'd say you would have been happy eating alone." When he didn't contradict me, I continued. "Why ask me to join you?"

He leaned forward, folding his hands together and placing them on the table. "You seemed like you could use my assistance. Besides, I found the idea of eating alone this evening oppressive. I'm glad you took me up on my offer."

"So am I."

Sebastian sat back in his chair, sipped his wine, and scanned the room. I did the same. My target wasn't present. I'd memorized everything in the file I'd been given when I took the assignment, particularly his appearance. If Alexander Holden was as low-key as it mentioned, then eating here would not be his thing. It sure wasn't mine. I was grateful for our discreet location, where we could watch without being noticed.

Five tiered chandeliers hung from the ceiling, their crystals catching candlelight and casting rainbow reflections along the crown molding and pale yellow walls. Floral arrangements dominated each corner of the room, including ours. The strong scent of citrus mingling with gardenia came from the vase of Lady of the Night orchids directly behind me. My attention wandered to the self-absorbed clientele and back to Sebastian. His gaze settled on the entryway. He frowned, took a larger sip of his wine.

"I don't know if I should be offended or not," I said, drawing him back to the here and now.

"I'm terribly sorry. How rude of me."

"No worries. I'm guessing you're looking for a

particular woman. One you thought would be here and you had hoped to make jealous by bringing me, dressed as I am, to dinner."

A bit of color flushed his cheeks. I'd hit a sore point.

"Yes. It seems you've found me out. I'm a true scoundrel. You should stay away from me, if you value your virtue." His tone was half-joking with an undercurrent of real warning.

I laughed. I'd lost my virtue a hell of a long time ago. Our food arrived, and we were spared any further comments on the subject. I was beginning to enjoy coming to dinner after all, despite Alexander Holden being a no-show.

It turned out that Sebastian's version of blood pudding was more like fresh roadkill. Very bloody. Not much filler and unrecognizable as to what it may have been in its former life. It also turned out I liked it.

We finished our meal, and Sebastian did another quick scan of the room.

"She would have been here by now," he said, then shrugged. "At least it hasn't been a total loss this evening. You've made dinner a more pleasant event. Thank you for indulging me."

"My pleasure."

"What about the person *you* had hoped to encounter?"

I coughed, sucking wine into my windpipe, which made me cough even more. It took a few moments to catch my breath. A few more until I could answer. "I suppose it's pointless to deny it."

"Boyfriend?"

"No. No. Nothing like that. He and I have a common acquaintance, and I was hoping to pass along the regards." I stumbled through my response, not sure I convinced him and not sure what to tell him. "His not being here is a disappointment, but I'm sure we'll connect before my stay ends." Somehow saying I was a bounty hunter didn't seem like a good idea, but I didn't want Sebastian to think I was trying to lure a straying boyfriend back to my bed either.

"How about a drink? We can finish our evening at the bar." His movements were smooth, fluid, purposeful as he led me down the grand staircase to the bar on the main level.

"More scouting?" I said, "Pretend we're here for a casual drink, a bit of flirting, all while we scope out the place." I wrapped my arm more firmly around his.

"Why, Mademoiselle Janda, I do believe you're mocking me."

"Not at all. I'm enjoying your tactics." I gave his arm a little squeeze. "Let's hope this works."

We entered a room that harkened to the Prohibition Era of speakeasies and lavishly dressed patrons and found two seats at the bar. The lighting was dimmer here than in the dining hall, but the decor was just as elegant. A mirror made up the length of the wall opposite us with an array of bottles laid out on a shelf at its base. My initial scan of the room for Holden wasn't promising, and my hopeful mood evaporated. The bartender approached us. She was dressed in a strapless evening gown of emerald green silk—apropos for the atmosphere the room invoked.

"Selena, my dear," Sebastian said, "how are you this fine evening?"

Selena could have been a runway model. Her long black hair hung in loose waves upon her olive-skin shoulders and flowed past the silk fabric covering her breasts.

"I'm well, darling Sebastian. And you?" She spoke in English, but with a mild accent that only added to her mystique.

"I am excellent. How could I not be? I have two beautiful women before me, and the night is young." His tone was teasing, and she ate it up.

"Stop. You're embarrassing me." Her eyelids fluttered beguilingly at her admirer. She'd been busy placing two shots of whiskey on the bar top—the movement so practiced I hardly noticed.

"This is Mademoiselle Janda. We met at dinner."

Selena reached out to shake my hand, a gesture I hadn't expected. "Pleased to meet you," she said. Her handshake was firm, her skin soft. She gave me a knowing, unsettling stare that had me pulling away from her touch.

"Likewise," I said. I wasn't sure I was pleased, but politeness dictated I agree. I placed my hands in my lap. The drink could wait until she was an arm's length from me.

Sebastian was unabashedly surveying the room for his lady friend, leaving me to strike up a conversation with Selena.

"Have you worked here long?"

"Yes."

She didn't elaborate. I tried again. "So, I guess you see a lot of people come in and out of your bar.

Gives you a chance to meet all sorts of supernatural beings."

She cocked her head to one side in thought. "Yes, I do suppose it does." She looked me in the eye. "Like you, for instance."

Not the direction I was hoping for. "Um. Right." I flashed her my smile. One more and I'd have a new record for most smiles in a day.

Sebastian saved me from further embarrassment by joining in the conversation. "Janda's a peach, Selena. A huge help in my endeavor this evening, but alas to no avail." He put a cold hand on my arm. "Sorry, no offense intended. You've been wonderful, but I'm afraid my expectations for meeting my friend have been dashed and I can't bear to ruin the rest of your evening by moping." He sent goosebumps running up my arm at his cool touch.

"Please. Your company has been the best part of my day." I meant it, too. Sebastian's presence seemed to lift my spirits and make my failure to find Alexander Holden more tolerable.

"Too kind." He brought my hand to his lips, kissed it gently, and held it between his hands. "Adieu, sweet Janda. I hope you find what you're looking for."

He seemed even colder than before, but that might have been my imagination. I was thrown by his reference to what and not who. What would I find in this strange place?

"I bid you both goodnight." He pecked Selena on the cheek and left.

Selena let out an airy breath. "The poor dear."

"Is Sebastian okay?"

"No."

Again, she didn't elaborate. Holding an intelligent conversation was seeming less and less likely. Time to find an excuse to leave. I understood Sebastian's frustration in not finding his friend. I had to find my target soon or risk losing the contract, but I wasn't the moping type. I hadn't figured Sebastian to be that type either. What concerned me was his physical state. The guy was like an ice cube.

"You seem to know Sebastian pretty well. Can you tell me if he's always so cold?"

Selena was silent. Maybe I shouldn't stick my nose in where it didn't belong. I should have learned that by now. No good came from messing in other people's business. When she still didn't answer, I decided to take my leave. "Thanks for the drink," I said and put my hands out to push my chair away from the bar.

She grabbed my arm, and I froze. "No, he's not okay. You can help him. He's sick." She gazed into my eyes, still holding my arm, and seemed to come to a decision. "The woman he was to meet was someone who might have been able to help him. He's been waiting for her to arrive for quite some time."

"I just met him, and you say I can help. What exactly is wrong with him?" I had a niggling in my stomach, which generally wasn't a good omen.

"I have a gift," she said.

"That's . . . nice." This was getting weird. I wasn't about to take any gifts from her. I tugged free, but didn't leave. I liked Sebastian. I wanted to know more about his situation. Selena rounded the bar and took a seat next to me. I sat back on my stool.

"I know what you are, Janda."

Her lips compressed to a thin line, and everything about her indicated she was serious, but I couldn't begin to guess how she would know I was a Lykoi.

"Your gift tells you what I am," I said, disbelief evident in my tone. I wanted her to tell me who had tipped her off. When I found out, that person would be asking Santa for a new set of teeth for Christmas.

"Yes." Her lips softened, resuming their natural plumpness.

"Right. Care to explain how this gift works?" I pushed her a little more.

"I can't."

I thought as much. She was getting insider information and using it to con her customers. As if she could read the doubt in my mind, she sat up straighter, a defiant posture I was all too familiar with myself.

"I can't explain, because I don't actually know how it works," she said, her voice even, firm, not a quaver of deceit in it. "It's something I was born with, just as you were born a mixed breed, a Lykoi."

I also sat up straighter, chin up in defiance, then did my best to relax. It seemed I wasn't the only one with an emotional trigger point. "We don't choose what we're born to be," I said.

"Very true." She also relaxed a tad. "My gift is tactile. When I touch someone, I sense their inner strength, and what they are becomes apparent. Almost like a vision." She shifted in her seat, smoothing the wrinkles in her dress, before meeting my gaze. "I know there's more to you than even you are aware of, and I don't make such claims lightly.

You are a force of nature that has yet to find its true purpose, but you will."

"How philosophical. Excuse me if I don't share your belief. I live a more practical life. What you're saying is of no consequence to me, and I'm at a loss as to what this has to do with Sebastian."

She smiled indulgently. "It has everything to do with Sebastian."

I waited, and she took her time continuing with her narration.

"Sebastian is an old soul."

"I agree." I'd sensed it with his politeness and old-world manners. Sebastian was not of my time. That much was clear.

"Do you?" She nodded. "Yes. I see you do. You're sensitive to weakness, and you detected it in him. That's the predator in you."

I wouldn't deny it. I was good at my job because I was a good hunter.

"You felt his body temperature drop. He's sick. You sensed that too, I'm sure. However, what makes you a great predator isn't just the way you can detect someone's weakness. It's your willingness to take risks."

"My uncle calls that being reckless. He's tried to squelch that in me, but it's not something I seem to be able to control."

Selena laughed, a high tinkling like music from wind chimes. "I'm glad he wasn't successful. I need the risk-taker in you to prevail. If you're willing to take a chance on Sebastian, I believe you can cure what ails him. It's in your blood."

She was entering dangerous territory. Discussing

my heritage was something I didn't do. It was akin to taking the family skeletons from the closet and parading them around town. It wasn't done.

"What's my blood have to do with his illness?"

"He's a vampire. An ancient one. He's developed a disease that requires an antibody not found in normal creatures. It's quite rare. The woman he'd been waiting for tested positive for it—a recessive trait and not overly strong, but the closest we'd found—and she'd agreed to be a blood donor." Her face fell slightly. "I don't know why she didn't show up."

"So now you want me to donate my blood?" I said, meeting her gaze. "Sorry. I'm rather partial to keeping as much of it in my body as possible. I can see why this woman may have had second thoughts."

"You wouldn't need to give it all to him."

"Well, that's a relief." I layered my words with a hefty dose of sarcasm. Her tone implied I would be required to give up more than was probably healthy for me and I couldn't afford to be weakened—not when I had to bring in Alexander Holden.

Selena wasn't fazed a bit. "Good. Then I will make the necessary arrangements and we can proceed in a few hours with the transfusion."

"Hold on. I didn't agree to do this."

"I noticed Sebastian wasn't the only one searching for someone. You didn't find who you were looking for either."

I clenched my jaw, and every part of me tensed. Selena's gift was a formidable one. She was far too astute at reading people and finding their vulnerabilities. Selena was a predator of a different sort.

"Your point is?"

"I can help you. I'm a bartender. I see and hear many, many things from those I encounter. You help Sebastian, and I will help you." Her eyes glistened with glee.

She had me, and she knew it.

CHAPTER FOUR
Blood Lust

Selena was true to her word, at least as far as the arrangements went for Sebastian's treatment, which I still had my doubts about. She'd assured me I'd never be pressured into something I wasn't comfortable doing. I was already uncomfortable. Yet there was also a part of me that was curious about what could make Sebastian ill. Sick immortals? It made them more human to me, even though they had lost their humanity the day they became vamps. I had to know more. Probably the cat in me surfacing.

The procedure room, as Selena called it, was a relatively small space given the grandness of everything else in the Hotel, but it felt homey. It was clean, but not in a stark, sterile way. There were no hospital gurneys and no harsh lights. Two divans had been placed next to each other near a blazing marble fireplace. Softly scented candles had been scattered around the room. I breathed in the distinct smell of Douglas firs' light geranium mixed with a hint of lemony pineapple—a natural stress reliever.

"Thank you for coming." Sebastian stepped out from the shadows of a bookcase with a leather-bound book in hand. I couldn't see what he'd been reading because the spine and cover were so worn any lettering that might have once existed had disappeared. It was the size of a small journal, and the way he tucked it inside his jacket made me think it was indeed personal.

I took a few steps forward. "Where do you want me?"

He relaxed his posture, swept his arm in the direction of the divans and allowed me to make the first move. He seemed like the Sebastian from our dinner, a gentleman from bygone days and not the ancient predator I now knew him to be.

"Either will be fine," he said. "You choose."

He followed behind me, but not too close. He seemed to know exactly how far he could go without spooking me. I chose the one nearer to the fire. Vamps could burn, and I wouldn't hesitate to snatch a log from the flames and torch his ass if things turned ugly.

The door opened, and Selena strode in, pushing a medical cart loaded with tubes and long syringes. My heart thumped out a succession of rapid-fire beats. I hated needles—a phobia I picked up in my youth. I could handle any amount of blood, watch prey get ripped into pieces, yet I had trouble with needles—go figure.

Sebastian glanced at me, and I was pretty sure he'd detected my anxiety. I mustered a calm I didn't feel. He removed his jacket, settled onto the other one, and leaned back on the stack of pillows. His position exposed his carotid artery. He rolled up his sleeves until his bare arms took on the same blue tinge as his face and neck. He'd made himself vulnerable to an attack, showing me he meant no harm and I was the one in control.

Selena had changed from her strapless number to a long-sleeve white cotton blouse and a matching skirt that came to the top of her art deco leather shoes she'd tied with a perfect bow. Her hair was pinned in a coiled bun. She'd gone from bartender to nurse with ease. It made me wonder if at some point she'd been a war nurse. She moved with precision and confidence as she arranged the equipment.

"This won't take long." Her tone reassured and soothed. Another sign of experience.

"How much of my blood will you need?" They both had been careful not to be specific.

"As much as it takes, but not so much as to incapacitate you." She popped the protective cover off a syringe she'd attached to a rubber tube. The tube had been affixed to a clear jar. I'd be able to see my blood being collected. I shifted my position a little nearer the fire.

"How will you know it's working?"

"I'll be able to tell you that," Sebastian said, "and as soon as I start to feel it take hold, I'll let you know."

"If it doesn't work? What then?"

Sebastian shrugged. "I die."

I didn't point out that technically he was already dead. There was dying, and then there was *dying*. I guess he preferred the former version. I could hardly blame him.

I narrowed my gaze at Selena. "Whether he lives or not, you still help me connect with my contact." I'd figured out pretty fast that the only way I'd locate

Alexander Holden was if I had help. I wasn't doing this out of the goodness of my heart. I liked Sebastian and wished him no ill will. I also liked my blood where it was—inside me.

"That was the agreement," Selena said. "I always keep my word."

"Just making sure we're on the same page." I sank deeper into the pillows and extended my arm. The veins stood out against my skin and pulsed rhythmically. "I'm ready."

Sebastian had been eyeing my vein. His fangs clicked into place. I should have been scared. I should have had better sense than to come, but the Hotel wasn't going to give me what I wanted without me paying a price.

He covered his mouth with his hand. "My apologies. It's the bloodlust. The reaction is unavoidable, but I won't attack. We'll do this Selena's way."

"Thank you," Selena said.

She was getting ready to stick me with the syringe. I sat up. "Wait. Selena's way? What other way is there?"

Selena sighed. "This is the medically approved method for blood transference between individuals. Yes, it may be a little less effective, but it should work."

"Hold up." I had a few questions that needed answering. "Medically approved method? Should work?"

She put the cover back on the syringe. "It seems a more detailed explanation is in order."

"Damn right. I still don't know what's wrong

with him."

Sebastian actually grinned. A glint of mischief flickered in his dark eyes.

"Lack of emotional gratification." That's all he said before Selena interrupted.

"Myths and legends meant to derail actual science." For the first time since I'd met her, she seemed agitated and annoyed.

"Calm yourself, dear Selena. I will do this however Janda prefers, but you know my preference."

She stared down at me. "Sebastian suffers from a condition we as yet don't understand completely. We only know that he's spent a number of years abstaining from his natural predilections in an attempt to satisfy the Accords. In other words, he drinks bottled blood and forgoes direct access to his donors."

"I was growing too powerful, which made for poor politics," he said. "You can't have a single person with more power than those in charge. You see, Janda, all of us paranormal beings have been fighting each other for as long as we can remember. The Accords are supposed to bring us together and keep peace, mainly by leveling the field. I didn't realize what I was giving up. Vampires need the physical experience we get from our donors." He shook his head. "I made a stupid bargain, and now I'm paying for it."

Selena's harsh tone softened. "He's been a man of his word. I respect that. He's also old-school and believes the bottled blood lacked the essential elements vampires crave—emotions—and that's why the disease set in. I and those like me are of a more scientific mind and think it's some sort of reaction to the preservatives used. We theorize that someone with your particular blood will provide the necessary antigens to fight the disease. Unfortunately, finding someone of your type has proven difficult."

"What exactly is my type?" I was sick of the attitudes I encountered about mixed breeds—of profiling and prejudice—and of letting it roll off my back, as I'd been raised to do. Selena, though, seemed to have a more factual interest, so I bit back my grievances to see where she was going with this.

"Mixed breeds of unusual pairings create new antigens. His disease has grown resistant to the standard combinations and his immortality is slowly eroding. We of the scientific community believe a transfusion from a new source would force his body to respond to the disease. Furthermore, it should work perfectly well using medically proven techniques."

Sebastian waved casually in my direction. "There you have it. Nature vs. Science. You decide."

"Well, yes, that is the sum of it," Selena said. "I guess you can tell Sebastian prefers the hands-on approach. If you get my meaning."

I did. He wanted to suck my blood.

Selena rearranged the syringes on the tray. The clanking grated on my nerves. I hadn't thought much about Science vs. Nature, but I empathized with Sebastian. There was something about contact with prey that elevated my hormone levels and made me feel alive. Of course, when I hunted I didn't just drink my prey's blood. I devoured flesh, gnawing it from the bones. The occasional salad aside, I was a carnivore. I, however, didn't feast on humans. I stuck to the normal food chain.

I found it hard to put myself in Sebastian's shoes and be forced to live as he had once the deal was struck with the Accords. My whole life I went about my business—and my pleasure—without a thought to the political powers that governed the non-human population. My uncle shielded me from the impact of politics, and only now did I realize how difficult it must have been for him to raise me—a crossbreed, a half-blood anomaly—with the weight of the Accords bearing down on him. I was a product of the Accords. A union of opposing forces that from the beginning of time had been adversaries. While the Accords proclaimed sanctity of life and equality for all, it was a different story to live with the result of such a coupling and say it was okay. Old ways died hard.

Sebastian stared at me, his expression neutral. He was born of the old ways, I of the new. I made up my mind.

"Forget science. Sebastian and I will do this the way nature intended."

"You can't be serious." Selena's mouth gaped open.

"Very."

While Sebastian hadn't altered his expression, his eyes told me exactly how he felt. Relief, excitement, anticipation. He was easy to read. Still, he continued to let me lead this mad adventure. He sat up, back straight, arms by his side. Then he waited.

"I want a guarantee that using the natural method

won't bind me to a vampire. Otherwise, the deal's off."

"It takes more than a simple bloodletting to create such a link," Sebastian said. "You have my word of honor that you won't be blood-bound to me."

I considered what he said and whether he was lying. I also weighed the chances of me finding my target without help.

"If you think I'll be party to what you're about to do, you're wrong," Selena huffed. She gathered the equipment onto the cart and started across the room.

"Wait." I might be willing to give myself over to nature's way, but I wanted someone nearby to intervene if necessary.

"Changed your mind?" Sebastian said.

"No, but I would like Selena's presence." I didn't think I needed to spell it out for her, but she didn't budge. Even if my life depended on it, which it might, I wouldn't beg her to stay.

She pursed her lips. "Fine."

I breathed a sigh of relief.

"This doesn't negate our deal. I expect you to arrange a meeting between me and my contact." I wasn't about to let her out of this room without reaffirming our bargain.

She bristled. "The arrangements have already been made. As soon as you're done here, assuming you survive the natural method, you can meet Mr. Holden."

Selena was a woman of surprises. "I don't recall telling you who I'm meeting."

"I'm a bartender. I hear a lot of things."

"Apparently the walls talk, because no one knows

my business except me."

Both Sebastian and Selena chuckled.

"The Hotel is quite knowledgeable, and it finds ways to let us know what we need to know," Selena said. "You'll see that for yourself before long."

Here we were back to the Hotel having a will, a mind of its own. I'd seen quite a few odd things in my life, so who was I to balk at what she said now? If it was true, then I had to make sure the Hotel worked for me and not against me.

I glared at the two of them. "I expect I will. However, in this room, here and now, we make the decisions, and I choose to complete our transaction. Once it's done, you will fulfill your part and make sure Mr. Holden and I meet."

"Absolutely." She took a seat in a wingback chair, folded her hands on her white-skirted lap, and looked at me expectantly.

I turned my attention to Sebastian. "How do you want to do this?"

At first he seemed awkward, unsure of himself. I used my smile again, encouraging him. He reached for my hand, drew me over to his divan, and we sat there inches from one another. My wariness of his self-control lessened. Sebastian was a patient and gentle man. He brushed a finger lightly along my arm. A tingling of anticipation stirred within me. He caressed my cheek, my jaw, my neck. This was a dance of seduction, of mutual respect, and consent on my part.

I glanced at Selena to let her know I was fine. She situated herself at an angle in the chair, all the while maintaining eye contact with me. She had me covered. That's what I needed to know before relinquishing control. I gave myself over to Sebastian's attentions. He eased me onto my back, still stroking my bare arm and lulling me into a state of peace. He placed his cheek against mine, and even his sweet breath created an air of serenity I couldn't resist.

I didn't feel his fangs when they penetrated my skin. Nor was there pain as he drew blood from my vein. He hesitated but once, long enough to run his tongue delicately down my neck. The eroticism nearly made me climax. I wanted him in every way, yet he kept his composure and control, never once overstepping the unspoken boundaries between us. He bit again. I arched into him, pressing hard, urging him for more. He wrapped me in a tight embrace as spasms quaked through my body and he sucked harder.

Slowly my mind became my own again and I realized he'd stopped drinking. He'd sealed the wound when he ran his tongue along the area, then pulled a quilt over me while I shook from the experience. I couldn't stand, let alone run. He was a master huntsman. I was his quarry and I enjoyed the experience.

"Was it good for you, too?" I whispered, because even my voice quivered with the effort of speaking.

His eyes glistened with mirth. "Need you ask?"

"Just making sure it worked."

"I think it did. I won't know for sure until the symptoms improve, but if this was my last meal, I can assure you I will die a happy man."

It occurred to me that he could be in trouble with

the Accords for doing this, and I could too as his accomplice. "Does this break your agreement with the Accords?"

Selena answered for him. "No. The Hotel Paranormal is outside any jurisdiction. An inter-dimensional plane is a loophole many of our guests enjoy . . . for various reasons."

There was a smugness to her words that would normally have irritated me, but I was rather lethargic at the moment and could not have cared less.

"As soon as you've recovered, take the elevator to the green space. We call it the Green Room. You'll find Mr. Holden there. The rest is up to you." She pushed the cart to the doorway, then paused. "For your sake, Sebastian, I hope this works."

There was an underlying threat I didn't understand, but Sebastian took it in stride.

"I rest easy with my decision. You have no worries from me," he said.

Selena shut the door behind her with a bit more force than necessary. The exchange meant more to them than me, and I didn't see the point in pressing them for details.

Sebastian poured me red wine that tasted heavily of oak and warmed me from the inside out. I threw off the quilt and sat up. The room spun. I ducked my head between my knees and took a deep breath.

"Easy now. Slow down. You don't have to dash off so soon. Mr. Holden will be there."

"How do you know?" I spoke to the floor for fear of raising my head and passing out.

"Because, my dear Janda, Selena promised and the Hotel provides for its guests as it sees fit."

He put a cool cloth on the back of my neck and massaged my shoulders. I still had a little wine left in my glass, and with no straw to be had, the only recourse was to sit up and hope the spinning stopped. I drank every drop of my wine and didn't complain when Sebastian poured a another glass. I felt heady, but at least the dizziness had ceased. The foggy sensation could have been from the blood loss or the wine. More than likely it was both.

"Thank you," he said. "I am in your debt."

"You don't owe me anything. I made a deal with Selena, and that's payment enough for me." I didn't mention how sensual I found the experience to be. Under different circumstances I might find myself in bed with Sebastian. He was good. I suppose being immortal had its benefits, like perfecting one's skills.

He sat forward in his chair, his hands on his thighs and began strumming his fingers. He had the look of someone who was considering his next move in a game of chess. I don't play chess, but I know that look.

He stopped his strumming and took another drink, swirling the liquid around the glass. "If you don't mind me asking, what is Mr. Holden to you? Certainly you wouldn't have agreed to be my donor if all you were doing was passing along a message from a mutual acquaintance."

I tensed as much as two glasses of wine permitted. I wasn't offended by his bluntness, but it seemed like a good time to leave. "Sorry. I don't do pillow talk." I rose and headed for the door.

He placed his own unfinished glass of wine on an end table and raised one hand in a half-hearted gesture to stop me. "Please. I wouldn't dream of insisting you tell your secrets. Forgive me. I don't mean to interfere. I'm concerned that you might not know what you're getting into with him. Selena isn't the only one who hears things."

I stopped with my hand on the door handle. The knob's intricate scrollwork would probably be imprinted on my palm with how hard I gripped it. "What things?"

"Have a seat." He pointed to the chair Selena had vacated across from his divan.

I sat facing him. "What things?" I repeated, drawing out the words, emphasizing each consonant. Besides hating needles, I hated surprises. If he had information on my target, I wanted it.

Sebastian picked up his glass and took a long sip of wine. He twirled the stem in his fingers. The firelight cast a golden glow on his skin, which to my keen eyes appeared less blue and more yellow, as though jaundiced. I started to worry he'd keel over right in front of me, but he didn't seem to be in any discomfort.

"Mr. Holden is a formidable adversary. One you should approach with caution."

"He's not an adversary. Besides, I can take care of myself."

"While I'm certain you are more than capable of doing just that, I assure you this man will not go with you of his own free will."

"Who says I want him to go with me?" I brushed a strand of hair from my eyes to give my hands something to do. I was getting nervous that he might have somehow accessed my thoughts when he bit me, although I couldn't see how that could happen.

"Perhaps I was wrong about that aspect," he said, "but there have been others who have tried to take him from the Hotel. Most never reach the front door. Two, including a woman, have gotten close to him. Neither succeeded in persuading him to leave. Both were escorted out by security."

This was news to me and information my employer seemed to have thought I didn't need to know. Shit. Here I was thinking getting through the portal at Mutther's was the hard part of this bounty hunter case.

"I want to talk to him. After that, we'll see what happens. I'm here for two days. Most of my first day has been frittered away trying to catch sight of him. I agreed to Selena's proposition so I could meet him today. Unless you have something more than a warning to give me, I think it's time for me to go."

"I wouldn't want to keep you. However, there is something else you should know about Mr. Holden."

"That would be what?" My agitation came through in my tone, and Sebastian noted it with one arched brow.

"On the surface, one might think Mr. Holden is a dangerous killer, and make no mistake, he is lethal, particularly in his panther form. He's a magnificent specimen. That, of course, is not what I feel is important for you to know, although it could be of interest to you and how you handle your meeting with him."

Sebastian met my gaze, and there was no glint of humor dancing in his eyes. I met his hard stare with one of my own.

"What you must know," he said, "is that Mr. Holden is innocent."

I blinked my surprise. He knew more about Holden than he let on. I sure as hell hadn't expected to hear this.

CHAPTER FIVE
The Green Room

Damn. That's all that ran through my mind as the elevator hopefully took me to the Green Room. Sebastian wouldn't divulge his source to back up his statement, which left me no further along on this goose chase than before. He figured he'd said enough and I'd be able to sort it out on my own. Thanks a lot, Sebastian. Vamps.

The elevator stopped, the doors slid open, and today was not my day.

Yes, what lay before me was green, just not a room. I stepped out into a freaking jungle. I groaned. The Hotel hated me, or else it just loved messing with me. I turned to get back on the elevator, but the doors shut and no matter how many times I pushed the button, it refused to open.

Somewhere in this dense vegetation was an exit door. I'd learned that all floors had one for fire-code reasons. You just had to discover where it was hidden or pray in case of an emergency it would make itself visible. I did a quick check of my immediate vicinity. Nothing but trees and vines. I started tapping on each tree and listening for any hollow sound that would indicate it might be the exit. Knocking on trees is slow work when you're hampered by wearing a dress, even the skimpy black number I still wore from dinner. Sebastian hadn't even gotten a drop of blood on it, and now I had to climb several times to reach what I thought was the outline of a door, tearing the dress in the process. I could imagine what my bill for incidentals would be when I checked out.

After another false lead, I took a moment to rest on a branch. I was not getting out of here tonight— that much was clear. I was hungry. I was weak from blood loss. I was pissed.

I leaned against the trunk, stretched my legs out on the limb, and closed my eyes. I felt a presence. Someone or something was watching me. I kept my eyes shut and used my other senses to search the space around me. A slight vibration traveled along my legs, and the faintest whisper of breathing came from directly above. I opened my eyes to a panther on a branch a few feet away. I did a dive to the ground, rolled upon impact, and readied myself to shift.

The panther was fast leaping on me, and pinning me to the ground. No way could I change now. He glared at me with penetrating golden-yellow eyes, then snarled a low warning. I'd been the underdog enough in my uncle's pack to know when to submit. The panther could have killed me already, and in not doing so, he gave me a chance to survive. I'd wait for an opportunity to either attack or escape. His choice. I was in a shitty mood, so I'd be happy to kill the beast if I could and be done with him.

He nudged my head with his muzzle, sniffing my hair. Running from a predator is a sure way to ramp up their killer instincts, so the fact he hadn't ripped me apart and seemed more curious than hungry meant this panther wasn't just a panther.

"Alexander Holden?"

He raised his head to stare at me, confirming my suspicions. Son of a bitch.

"Get off me!" I shoved at him as best as I could in my current position. He got the message and backed off. I sat up and tugged at the dress that was beyond repair. It hadn't covered much of my body before I'd destroyed it, and now it was akin to wearing a dust rag. *Wonderful.* At least the essential parts of me were more or less concealed, but I had no delusions about my appearance. I brushed off dirt and ran my fingers through my hair to loosen the tangles. Alexander Holden sat on his hind quarters and watched. I could swear that bastard grinned.

"Enjoy it now, buster, because it's the last peep show you'll get from me." I stood as gracefully as possible, which didn't go well, and raised my chin defiantly. I might be a mess, but I still had my pride.

"Well? Are you just going to sit there, or are you going to shift back so I don't have to do all the talking?"

He didn't move. I was tempted to shift too, but without a bond to tie us to one another, it would shut down any chance we had of communicating. I sighed. "Fine. I'll keep chatting, but feel free to shift any time and make this a real conversation."

Nothing. So that's how it was going to be. *Fantastic.* Problem was I didn't know what to say to him. In my scenario of our first encounter I pictured myself having had the opportunity to observe him from afar. I like to study my targets, spend time analyzing weaknesses. Staying under the radar until I'm ready is a specialty of mine. Nighttime predators tend to give me a wide berth, mainly because they don't know what the hell I am, and I can melt into the shadows pretty well.

Here in the Green Room's jungle, it was nearing dawn, or so it appeared, a time most nocturnal beings would settle down for a quiet nap, which made them vulnerable to my attack. In this fabricated environment I couldn't rely on the natural rhythms of nature. The actual time of day was anyone's guess. My usual options being limited, I had to find a way to win his trust and somehow convince him to go back with me.

In the past, I'd found the tactic effective, because many of my targets were spent, done with running and tired from the weight of guilt. Mind, not all my bounty hunter targets had a conscience. Those were the tricky ones. The ones I had to wait out and catch at their weakest to haul their asses back in for justice. Depending on whether or not Alexander Holden had a guilty conscience, I might be able to convince him to return with me. Whereupon I'd hand him over to his clan leader, who would then pay me my bounty fee as per our contract, and I'd leave town, and my pack, in a trail of dust.

I gritted my teeth at the complicated mess that was the Hotel. This was not going as planned. And worse, if I was to get out of the jungle, I'd need his help.

Alexander Holden rose on all fours, spun around, and ducked behind a tree. I had to admit to being impressed. Sebastian was right. Holden was a magnificent specimen. He exuded power and an agile grace befitting his status as second of his clan. He was slated to take over as leader, but I doubted that would happen now. I needed to get him out of here and back home. What took place after that wasn't my problem.

"Better?" He strode from behind the tree fully clothed.

"How did you manage that?" I was incredulous. No shifter I knew could pull off what he'd just done.

"Manage what?"

"Did you bring clothes with you? Surely you can't shift back fully dressed. Can you?" If I was honest with myself, I'd have to admit my curiosity in seeing him in the raw. Despite my disappointment that it didn't happen, he took my breath away. Alexander Holden stood at a solid six feet tall. After seeing his sleek animal form, I half expected him to sport a long haircut and a full beard. He had neither. His hair had been buzzed military style to equal his dark six o'clock shadow. His bronze skin contrasted his white cotton button down shirt that was open to expose his well-honed chest muscles and the beginnings of his six pack abs. Interestingly, he was bare-footed beneath his tight jeans. Cover model on a men's magazine came to mind.

He smirked. "The Hotel provides for my needs. It does for you as well, if you know how it works."

I frowned. At this precise moment my needs would not be fulfilled by the Hotel. "It must have been in the fine print. Guess I missed it when I checked in."

He came towards me exuding dominance, and I had to steel myself from stepping backward. He lifted his nose, sniffed the air around me.

"That's plain rude." I crossed my arms and glowered at him.

He didn't apologize. "You've been in close proximity to Sebastian."

I automatically touched the spot where Sebastian bit me, even though he'd sealed the wound and I was certain no sign of it remained. "What of it?" I was sure any supernatural in the area would have no trouble detecting a male scent on me after what I'd just done. I didn't care what others thought, and I had nothing to hide.

"You two must be very close for him to have marked you."

"Holy shit! He didn't!"

"He did."

I whirled around searching for the elusive exit. Sebastian might be dead already, but I was going to make sure he stayed good and dead. He'd promised there wouldn't be any blood ties, and Selena hadn't stepped in to stop him. What was he thinking? I paced along the tree line. I *so* wanted to kill something. An image of Selena as she was leaving the room replayed in my mind. Her conversation with Sebastian took on a new light. She knew what he'd done. And he had no remorse.

"You don't seem pleased," Holden said. "I'm guessing he did it without your knowledge, perhaps during an intimate moment when he thought you wouldn't notice."

I rallied my anger back at Holden. "That's none of

your business."

"So I'm right." His expression of wariness eased some. "You must have done him a great kindness for him to mark you."

I kicked at a clod of dirt just to release a minuscule amount of rising frustration. Nothing of this contract was working out. Somehow I had to pull my shit together and focus on my goal— Alexander Holden and my bounty fee. I closed my eyes and exhaled. It took another deep breath before I felt my muscles relax.

Holden scrutinized me several long moments. "He did you a favor, you know."

"No. I don't know, and he can just unmark me. I'm not his. I belong to no one but myself."

"Guess you haven't been claimed before because it's not that easy a thing to undo."

Holden was right. I'd never been claimed. No one had ever wanted me.

"Sebastian will fix it."

"You're assuming he would *want* to undo it, and I can tell you that you might not want to be too hasty to throw away the gift he's given you."

I came back over to Holden to get a better look at an insane person, because he had to be nuts to think being marked by a vampire was a gift. "What he did isn't a gift."

I couldn't mention that it would draw attention to me, and that I'd spent my whole life learning how not to be noticed. Sebastian had placed a bulls-eye on me for all those who loved to torment half-breeds.

"It kept me from accidentally hurting you. Sebastian is my friend, which by extension makes you a friend. He's a powerful figure. Anyone would be stupid to infringe on his territory, unless they want a quick and painful death."

It was true I'd seen several vamps hanging around the Hotel, but I'd been made aware of the rules. No harm could come to any of the guests. That didn't mean once I'd left the same would apply. I was well aware that the rules of the outside world were much harsher and only those smart enough or strong enough survived. Unless you had protection.

"I don't think any of that matters if I can't get out of this jungle."

"If you don't want to be here any longer, you could always take the elevator. Didn't you use it to get here?"

My irritation was growing. "Of course, but it wouldn't let me back on."

"Really?"

The gold in his eye grew more brilliant and more alluring. The skepticism in his voice, however, irked me. Like I had a choice in the elevator doing a dump and run.

"Yeah, really." I huffed.

"Then the Hotel thinks you should be here, as does Sebastian, considering he sent you."

The truth didn't seem like a wise direction to go. "The Hotel and I aren't on speaking terms. It prefers to toy with me instead. However, you seem to do better with it, so maybe you should ask it."

He belted out a roar of laughter. "I'll remember that next time."

"You know, I think I preferred you as a panther. At least then you couldn't say stupid things to tick me off."

In a blur of motion, he launched himself high in the air and landed on a thick branch. "That can be arranged. You can find your own way out, and I can go back to what I was doing before you interrupted. You can tell Sebastian thanks for trying, but it didn't work out."

I leapt towards the branch, grabbed hold of it, and swung myself up beside him. Not exactly as impressive as his maneuver, but it did the job. "Where you go, I go. At least until I find the exit door or the elevator lets me back on. Since the latter doesn't seem likely to happen, you're stuck with me." I tucked a shred of fabric into the edge of my bra. The dress strap had given way completely when I jumped into the tree.

"We'll see who's stuck. By the way, nice jump. The landing could use some improvement, but not bad." He straddled the branch, edging a little closer. "So you're not human. You have catlike abilities, but you're also something else. If I shift, how will you keep up? Change too? You're a shifter of some sort. That much I'm certain."

His voice held questions I wasn't ready to answer. I don't advertise being a Lykoi.

"I could be more than you imagined and much more than you could deal with. Do you really want to shift just to find out?"

"Maybe," he said. He stood and walked to the end of the branch until it bent from his weight, then hopped to the branch of another tree. He sat semi-hidden within its leaves. Vines of a hybrid hibiscus dangled in a curtain around his form, but he didn't shift.

I followed his lead to the next tree and stood in front of him, using a vine to hold myself steady. Dew from the flower petals sprinkled over my shoulders, dousing me in its strong perfume. "My name's Janda Gray. You can call me Janda or Gray. I answer to either."

"My friends call me Holden. Alex when they're pissed at me." He pushed away a vine. "I'm glad you came. I'm not sure how Sebastian thinks you can help me, but it's been a good distraction from the funk I've been in lately."

Christ, he thought Sebastian sent me to help him out. He couldn't be more wrong, and I was starting to feel guilty about it.

"Did Sebastian tell you I make safe rooms for a living? It's ironic, really. Imagine one of the best architects of such spaces hiding out in the biggest safe room imaginable — the Hotel Paranormal." He tore petals from a blossom and let them fall to the ground.

He didn't behave like the fugitives I usually dealt with in my bounty hunter cases. I couldn't figure him out, and that bugged the shit out of me. I offered him another kernel of truth. "Sebastian didn't go into a lot of details, but he insisted you were innocent."

He nodded. "He's a good friend that way."

Of course, the rest of what I knew came from Holden's clan leader, and all the evidence pointed to Sebastian being wrong. I worked for Silas, who was convinced his niece had been killed by Holden. I didn't think Silas would lie. The guy was devastated. He'd handpicked Holden to marry into the family and set him up to take over as leader. Werecat groups weren't like wolf packs. Silas's members abided by territorial rules and kept outsiders at bay but for the most part lived solitary lives, coming together in groups only for special events or mandatory meetings.

I could see why Silas was anxious to get Holden firmly ensconced in the familial fold. It would have solidified the clan's position in the state's paranormal community to have a powerful panther as their new leader. I wasn't big into politics, but I was acquainted with the undercurrents that ran through my world. It was imperative to have a strong leader who could speak for a group's rights on a state and national level, particularly with anything regarding the Accords.

Holden was perfect for the position. He just didn't want it. Not the title or the girl. Holden tore another blossom from the vine and shredded it, not in an angry way, but in a sad one.

Christ, this guy was getting to me in more ways than I cared to think about. A branch caught at his waist when he moved to jump from the tree, causing a gap between fabric and flesh. My breath hitched at the sight. He went commando, as evidenced by the healthy glimpse of ass being revealed.

I dropped to the ground but made sure to keep some distance between us. "Okay. I'm not sure what's going on, or how I'm supposed to help your case, but I need to leave. We can go into this more later." I was struggling with keeping my fabric scraps in place. I also had to re-evaluate this assignment. "Can you just show me the way out?"

He pointed in the direction of the elevator.

"Very funny," I said. "Been there. Done that. Remember?"

"Ah, but not with me you didn't." He sauntered over and pushed the button. The doors slid open.

I brushed past him. "I'm really beginning to hate you."

He laughed and followed me into the elevator from hell.

"I'd say we could go back to my room to discuss the case, but you probably want to change. How about your room instead?"

"Fine by me."

I concentrated on where I wanted the elevator to take us and hoped it knew what it was doing. I also hoped I knew what *I* was doing, because life had all of a sudden gotten a lot more complicated than a basic stalk and capture. I caught myself thinking of what it'd be like to see the rest of Alexander Holden's body. Very complicated indeed.

CHAPTER SIX
Innocence

"Athena, huh?" Holden followed the direction the statue pointed. "I got Janus. Try finding your way around the Hotel with a god whose head has two faces pointing in opposite directions."

I had to laugh. Couldn't help it. This place was seriously messed up. "I can see how that might be a problem."

"You have no idea." He leaned one hand against the wall by my room.

I fished out the rectangular key from where I'd hidden it under a bust of an armored Athena that sat on a marble stand beside my door.

"Key too big to carry?"

I ran a hand over the remnants of my dress. "You see any pockets?" Dresses weren't great for holding things, like keys and guns. My gun had been taken with my clothes, and the key wasn't important enough to worry about.

The yellow in his eyes brightened. "Point taken."

Holden had very expressive eyes. I didn't need a pack bond to know what he was thinking. I decided a few ground rules were in order before we entered. "Let's get things straight. One, this is a business meeting and not to be construed as anything else. It's business and nothing more. Two," I stared him straight in the eyes, "nothing more. Got it?"

He stared right back at me. "Got it."

He took a seat by the only table in the room, an oval coffee table positioned between two deep-cushioned chairs. I rummaged through the wardrobe, griping every few minutes as I rejected garment after garment. I gave up and chose a mini-skirt and sequined top. "I swear all they think I wear are clothes that say 'Come fuck me now.' Not a single pair of jeans, and worse, look at these." I held up red stilettos. "How do women walk in these things? Can you see me trying to ride my Harley wearing them? I'd kill myself." I threw the shoes into the back of the wardrobe closet. I *so* missed my leather boots.

"Harley, huh? I can picture you on one. Red shoes included."

"Why do I bother explaining myself?"

His demeanor held ample sex appeal that had me wondering what else he was picturing me doing. I grabbed the clothes and stalked off to the bathroom, my own version of the Harley scene playing in my head. I had an appreciation for finely built men, and so far this trip had given me plenty to admire. I had to admit Holden's dossier couldn't compare to the real deal, and I'd been duly impressed by what I'd seen in his file.

"The Hotel is a resort. It's meant for relaxation and play. Maybe it thinks you should loosen up. There's a terrific spa you might want to check out. I hear they offer special massages."

I could guess what 'special' meant. "I don't do

spas. I have my own ways of relaxing, and as far as play goes, I'd say from what I've been given to wear, the Hotel thinks *I'm* the plaything." I'd left the door ajar so I could hear if Holden was nosing about. There wasn't anything for him to find since I made sure to destroy everything before I came here. I poked my head around the door and caught him going through the wardrobe drawers. "Would you mind ordering breakfast? I'm starved."

He startled and dropped the lace bra he had in his hands. He quickly redirected and reached for the nearby phone. "I ate earlier, but tell me what you want and I'll order it." A hint of color darkened his face.

I smirked at his embarrassment. "I'd love a thick steak for starters, and anything else they want to send up."

I was dressed for an evening at a nightclub, not breakfast, but I didn't think Holden would care one way or the other. His suppressed smile proved me wrong, and like a silly schoolgirl, I enjoyed his response. There was something about this guy that made me wish I was the sexy, desirable type the Hotel portrayed me as being. I paused in the bathroom doorway, just realizing what he'd said. "You were hunting when I found you."

"Small game. And I like fish. I was heading to the river when you arrived."

"There's a river in the Hotel?" The building was huge from the outside, but a river?

"If you can imagine it, then it exists. The staff takes great pride in providing anything and everything for its guests. Ethically, of course."

"Of course." I also believed they weren't above bending those ethics. I'd been manipulated since the moment I got here. Once I was finished with my meeting with Holden, I was going to track down Sebastian.

Room service arrived in record time with steak and eggs and a pot of black coffee. They also brought in a respectable table to eat at and made fast work of setting everything up, including a white tablecloth and napkins. A bowl of fruit and a selection of pastries completed the morning banquet.

"I could get used to this," I said, cutting into the meat and watching the blood seep into the poached eggs. One bite and I was a convert to the establishment. "Okay, this Hotel seriously rocks. I think I'm in heaven."

"I can't take it," he said. "Let me have a bite."

"Weren't you the one who ate already and wasn't hungry?" I teased him by slowly chewing another morsel and even more slowly licking my lips.

"That's mean. And erotic. Are you sure you're not a professional hooker?"

"Food and sex. That's all men need to be happy."

He shrugged. "Not all, but it helps." He reached over, swiped a piece of steak, and popped it into his mouth. He closed his eyes as he ate, and when he was done, he let out a moan. "Oh, yes. You weren't kidding. This is amazing."

"Told you." I used a piece of toast to soak up the yolk and steak juices. I gave him a slice to do the same. "Dig in or I'll finish it off."

We shared the rest of the meal and groaned in utter satisfaction when we couldn't stuff ourselves anymore. He was a stranger to me, not to mention being my bounty prey, yet I was at ease with him. I chalked it up to the afterglow of a scrumptious breakfast.

Holden poured himself a cup of coffee. "That's the first prepared meal I've had since I got here. I've been catching my own food, but hell, this is damn good."

I shook my head in disbelief. "Why would you do such a thing?"

He sat the cup on the table. "I trust what I can see and catch myself."

"I get that. I do, but that makes no sense. The rules of the Hotel prohibit anything bad happening to you, so why be paranoid?"

"It's true I'm relatively safe here. However, rules can always be broken, or bent, especially when there's a price on your head. It doesn't matter if it's here or outside this pocket dimension. Shit happens."

I almost choked on my mimosa. If he had any inkling of why I was here I'd be screwed.

He pushed back from the table and faced me. "You ready to talk business?"

I switched out the alcohol for a cup of coffee. I'd been awake for over a day and was starting to feel the effects. Caffeine was a priority if I was going to get through the next few hours. "I am now."

"You said Sebastian didn't say much about my situation, but did he tell you I came to him for help?"

"No." It seemed I'd been good and played by that blasted vamp. I also recognized a foot in the door when I saw it. I could work with this. "Why don't you start at the beginning?"

Silence permeated the room. "Or not," I said. "Up to you." I topped off my cup. If he didn't open up now, I might never lure him into trusting me and I didn't have any other options. Plan A had been blown away pretty much right after I entered the Hotel. As a result, I was more than willing to let him believe Sebastian had sent me to help — my plan B.

Holden studied me, quietly assessing my abilities as near as I could tell. Or he was enamored with me, which was highly unlikely.

"I don't know what Sebastian was thinking you could possibly do for me?"

"I can't speak for Sebastian's thoughts," I said, "but I'm here and willing to listen. Guess you have to decide for yourself if I'm the right person for job. Just don't take long to figure it out. I leave tomorrow." I was guessing as to how much time I had left, because I didn't know how time worked here. It wasn't exactly like taking a road trip across the country and dealing with time-zone differences. I had no experience with any dimension but my own.

My departure news seemed to startle him. Our congenial atmosphere evaporated, and tension took its place. What happened next would be up to him and could determine the direction of my future. I twisted the napkin between my fingers.

"I suppose you might be useful," he said, more to himself than to me. "They wouldn't recognize you at least, so it might work." He tossed a half-eaten sticky bun onto his plate and licked his fingers clean. "All right, then. I'll fill you in on what I know."

I breathed a sigh of relief and curled up in the chair with my mug. "Enlighten me. I'm all ears."

"My clan leader, Silas Vang, has had a rough time recently. He's been talking retirement. It's unusual for a leader to retire, so it came as a huge surprise to the rest of us. What was more surprising is who he pegged to take his place."

"I'm guessing you."

"Not what I had planned to do with my life, I can tell you that. Being responsible for my employees is one thing, but watching out for an entire clan with families depending on you is totally different. And before you give me the second-in-command lecture, let me tell you that I'd agreed to the position because Silas's second died and he had to have someone to guard his back until he found the right person to take over. He had a couple of interested parties, his nephew for one, but last I heard Silas hadn't made a decision. I was a place-holder, not the permanent solution. I'm a corporate guy. I've worked hard building a successful business, and I don't want it to fail. The rich pay hefty fees for safe rooms but only when I can devote myself to my work and give them a superior product."

"I can imagine." Sarcasm was hard to hold in when I was staring at someone with a privileged existence. I didn't have much experience with having money, but I could still dream of how I'd live if I happened to win the lottery. Holden was my ticket out of low-income living and crappy-paying bounty hunter jobs. I enjoyed my line of work, but I'd retire in a heartbeat. Hell, that was why I was here.

"The point is," he said, "I'd have to change everything, maybe lose everything, to do what Silas wanted—marry his niece, become clan leader, and give him an heir."

"Sounds rough to be asked to take over a respected clan and have it boost your recognition. It could even get you more notice in the corporate world and land you more jobs, increase your income. You could afford to take on a business partner to help you out."

"I bet it sounds like a good life to you. Except it's not easy finding a partner you can trust. I've been down that road before." He frowned, and his tone darkened with the storm of emotions brewing within him. "Tell me. What would you do if someone set up an arranged marriage that you didn't want? And it could destroy all you'd fought hard to create for yourself?"

I scowled at the idea. "I'm not the marrying kind."

"Neither am I."

I uncurled my legs and sat up. "Okay. So you didn't want what he was offering. Why not tell him 'no' and be done with it?"

"I can't believe you're asking me that. You're a shifter. You have some kind of pack ties. How would you tell your leader 'no thanks'?"

I had to think about it for a while, because truth was I couldn't ever recall being asked to do anything for my uncle. He set the rules, I skirted the edges of them, he left me to my own devices. A pang of hurt hit me in the usual spot—my heart—for I realized it meant I didn't matter. I'd always known it, but somehow the constraints Holden had to face drove home how much of a nothing I was in my pack.

"I think it's best to stick with your situation, not

mine. What I want to know is if you say you didn't kill the woman you were to marry, then who did? And why would her death get you out of taking over as clan leader?"

"Accused killers don't win good-guy popularity polls."

"That's not an answer."

He let out a long, exasperated sigh that reminded me of the times I'd tested my uncle's patience.

"Murder tends to create a divide among clan members. Those from the old ways wouldn't bat an eye at me taking over after what happened. Death is part of life, especially when it comes to weeding out the weaker genes. They would have seen Myra as not strong enough to be the leader's mate. Then there are the others who want integration with the rest of the world and think the best way is to follow human laws. They'd want her killer turned over to authorities. Death and politics—a mess no matter how you view it. Now do you see the larger issue? I'm not making light of Myra's demise. I'm here to avoid breaking up my clan."

He leaned his head back and rubbed hard at the stubble on his chin. I could see by the lines beneath his eyes that he'd spent a number of sleepless nights since he'd left his home for the safety of the Hotel. Maybe my perp had a conscience after all. As much as I wanted to deny it, I believed he was telling the truth. In that moment my *Midnight Run*, that easy gig, evaporated.

He met my gaze with deep-set sadness, yet his clenched jaw showed barely contained anger.

"I saw her lifeless stare, and now I see her every

time I try to sleep. I didn't want to marry her—be bound to her. Now I can't escape her." He balled his fists. "When I find who killed her, I guarantee the person will be dealt the ultimate in clan justice."

This was the man I'd read about in his files. The person who rose above politics and treated his employees with kindness and generosity. He might say he didn't want to be responsible for others, but his actions proved otherwise. He'd be surprised to find how many were loyal to him and would follow him as clan leader. Silas had hired me to bring Holden back, but now I saw how his returning before Myra's killer was found would be detrimental to the clan.

I stood and began wearing a path in the carpet while I processed these additional facts. My exhaustion worked to fuel my agitation, and I itched for physical release.

Holden sprang from his chair and grabbed my hand as I made my next circuit. He tugged me in the direction of the bed, and my heart soared in anticipation. My bare legs brushed the bedcovers, sending ripples of sexual energy surging over my skin. The sensation abruptly fizzled when we continued in the direction of the door.

He reached for the doorknob. "Let's go."

I dug in my heels because that's my automatic response to anything I deem undermining my free will. I was big on making my own damn choices. "Where?" I planted myself more firmly in place. He released my hand.

"I'm tired of watching you pace, so I'm taking you to the river."

"The river?"

"Do you have to question everything?"

"Yes."

He rolled his shoulders and opened the door. "Stay if you want, but I'm going." He paused a fraction of a moment before striding out into the hall.

Panther or human, the guy presented an enticing view. I practiced my free will and followed.

Once in the Green Room, we rounded a bend in the path, and I gasped at the marvel before me. A small waterfall splashed into a wide pool before the river wound its way lazily out of sight. I wondered where it would end if I followed its path. It seemed so natural, so real, I had trouble reconciling that we were inside a building. Or were we?

"Are we still in the Hotel?"

"I've asked myself that question, but the truth is I don't know. Does our reality alter to meet our desires, or does the Hotel actually manifest our dreams? How does anything work in this place? It just does."

I kicked off my high-heels and stepped into the shallows, where cool water lapped at my legs. I closed my eyes and let the calm seep into my bones. Tiny splashes danced along my calves. Holden had come to stand next to me, his earthy scent stirring something deep within me that I'd never experienced before. Desire flared, and I had to remind myself of what he was to me—a job.

I opened my eyes, still soaking in the peacefulness of his river, for it was a manifestation of his that he'd offered to share with me.

"Thank you," I said. "It's incredible."

"Yes, it is."

He spoke with admiration and gratitude, and he was watching me, not our surroundings. Time to get back on track and away from emotions I couldn't afford to acknowledge. I moved to a boulder beside the water's edge and sat with my legs tucked beneath me. The mini-skirt was definitely mini. At least I'd thought to wear a thong. Underwear was a convention I usually did without—a shifter's reality.

"I've been going over what you said. Do you think Myra's murder was committed by a random killer and you just happened to take the blame— wrong place, wrong time?"

"I doubt it," he said, sitting next to me with his jeans rolled up and his feet dangling in the water. "We do a decent job of keeping tabs on strangers wandering into our territory, but what bothers me is I found her body on the line between our lands and the wolf domain. I was supposed to meet her in town to talk about our options. She wasn't keen on the marriage either but was willing to abide by her uncle's wishes. I got the impression she had her sights on some other guy, but Silas wouldn't have it."

Silas hadn't mentioned a possible lover or any of the territorial issues when he'd given me Holden's file. I was beginning to see a lot of holes in Silas's logic. "You think a wolf did it?"

"Possibly. There've been sightings of a rogue wolf beyond our borders. The pack leader in our area made sure we knew it wasn't one of theirs." He shrugged. "I did smell wolf on her, but it could have been from an earlier encounter. She drove a delivery truck for a distillery and made regular drops at various bars, some in wolf territory. None of them would dare lay a hand on her, though, so it doesn't add up."

"Let's view it from another angle and say it was an inside job. Who would benefit from her death?"

"No one."

"What if it was a way to set you up? Do you have any enemies?"

He laughed and tossed a stone that skipped along the water's surface. "I have plenty of enemies. It's part of the job description. Crooks don't like it when you build barriers between them and their wealthy targets. My systems have allowed the cops to catch intruders and put them behind bars. Another reason I'd prefer not to go there myself. I'd have to sleep with my eyes open to survive their revenge."

"If not a wolf, then what about closer to home? The nephew? He'd have a motive—get rid of you and secure his position in the clan."

"No way. Myra was his sister. He loved her. He's sworn to kill me on sight, but he'd have to catch me first and I don't plan on having that happen."

"Maybe we're looking at this all wrong. Myra's death could have been personal and nothing to do with you. If she became mate to the new clan leader, then what would happen to Silas's mate? A woman can kill just as easily as a man."

"Not a dead woman. She died in a car crash with his second—my brother." Holden's voice had dropped, and he tossed another stone into the water where it plunked into the depths.

"Sorry. I didn't know."

"It's been hard on all of us, especially Silas. He's

lost without his mate. A broken man is a weak one, and he knows it. Better to appoint a replacement and step aside than to risk a takeover by another clan. My presence was meant to give him time to make the best decision for the clan and keep other greedy leaders from expanding into our territory. Like I said, politics and death."

"Another clan vying for a takeover would make sense only if their actions guaranteed you would be ousted. You don't need a wife to be leader. You could take one later, on your own terms, so that brings us back to the beginning. Who benefited from her death, and why implicate you?"

Holden scooped a handful of water and splashed it over his face. "If destabilization is the goal in preparation for a takeover, then forcing me out of the picture would only be the first step. They'd have to eliminate any replacement possibilities. Damn. I have to warn Myra's brother. He could be next."

"You mean the brother who swore to kill you? That brother?"

"Leon thinks I strangled his sister because I didn't want to marry her. Can you blame the guy for wanting me dead?"

I didn't have to think long about it. "I see your point. I also think going back would be a stupid move. Heroic in a way, but stupid."

He grinned. "That's why *you're* going to tell him."

"What! No way!"

"You pointed out I can't go. Someone has to. You can slip in and out before they know you're there."

I waved my hand at him. "No. Absolutely not."

"You have to."

"No, I don't. And do you recall the part about you guys staying on top of strangers entering your territory? I'm not exactly part of the family, am I?"

That gave him pause, but not for long. "You could go on the pretense of mediating my surrender."

Holy fuck. I came to the Hotel to get him to surrender, and here he'd suggested it himself. There had to be a catch. The gods had never handed me anything on a silver platter before, and I wasn't sure I wanted them to now.

"You're insane. What exactly would I say to Leon? 'By the way, someone's out to get you, but I don't know who. And you may or may not be attacked, but you better watch your back.' A bit vague, don't you think? With no way of saying which direction the danger would come from and who's behind it, how would anyone believe me?"

"Leon doesn't need to believe you. The seed of doubt is enough to keep him on his toes and alive until we can find the real killer."

"We? You here and me there? How's that going to work?" I could think of a dozen scenarios in which I would be hung out to dry once they found out Holden had no intention of turning himself over to them. Holden, on the other hand, would extend his cushy stay at the Hotel Paranormal. I could feel my bad luck returning. It seemed no matter how this played out my bounty contract would be null and void.

I spent several moments looking Holden over. This jungle oasis must be messing with me. The lush greenery, the babbling water, his tawny muscles flexing with each stone he threw. He was everything I would have wanted—if my life was normal—and I wished nothing more in this moment than to be in his arms, savoring his kisses. Stupid me. I believed his story and his innocence. If I succeeded in proving it, I'd be giving away my financial freedom and guaranteeing I'd never be able to sever my pack ties unless Holden claimed me. Assuming I could clear his name, would he even want me afterward?

Not likely. I was a Lykoi. I was a mixed breed. I was a nobody.

CHAPTER SEVEN
Ties

We took the elevator back to my floor with the intention of me getting some rest while Holden sought Selena's help with accessing a portal that wouldn't take me to Mutther's bar and land me in the middle of a pack of wolves. The doors opened to Athena, and I swear a smile spread mischievously across her marble face as she pointed to my room — a blatant hint I tried to ignore.

"I'll wake you when everything is set."

He slipped a hand around my neck and drew me to him, exactly how I'd fantasized while we were sitting by the waterfall. His kiss unleashed a primal desire I'd always kept in check, yet I didn't care that it had surfaced and betrayed my deep-seated emotions. I relished every moment, lengthening the kiss, encouraging him by pressing my body against his. Neither of us seemed to want to break the spell we were under, but he released me, both of us breathless with desire.

"Amazing," he said, his voice deep and husky.

"I agree." I smiled at him, and for the first time I could remember it was fueled by natural, unfettered joy.

He nudged me gently out of the elevator. My feet moved of their own volition because the rest of me was still in lust mode. The cool air in the hallway brought me to my senses enough to articulate what I was thinking.

"I don't know how you expect me to be able to sleep now." I gave him a sly grin. "Maybe we should finish what we started and then you can find Selena."

He groaned. "You're killing me. I want to, but if we do we'll never leave your room." He stepped from the elevator and planted a quick kiss on my forehead. "We'll pick this up later. I promise."

"I'll hold you to it."

He returned to the elevator, the doors shut, and still I didn't move. Elation tainted by regret kept me rooted to the spot, staring at the swirled grain within the door panels. How could I have let this happen?

Holden's plan, its likelihood of success slim, hinged on me. Guilt riddled every fiber of my being. He still thought Sebastian had sent me, and I couldn't admit the truth. If Holden learned I was a bounty hunter hired by his clan leader, I'd be kicked out of the Hotel, or worse, he'd find a way to bend the rules and kill me.

I slunk back to my room and dropped onto my bed fully dressed. Sleep refused to come, and after an hour of lying there staring at a mural of naked cherubs on the ceiling directly over me, I gave up and headed for the bathroom. I ran the bathwater until the mirrors steamed up and I could no longer see my Judas image. I stripped, tossed the mini-skirt and top on the floor, then sank into the bath and dipped my head beneath the surface.

When I could no longer hold my breath, I emerged from my self-pitying submersion determined to salvage the mess I'd created. I'd allowed my own yearnings to take root and deluded myself about the real reason I'd come for Holden. Sebastian and Selena may have manipulated me, but if I was honest with myself, I had to acknowledge it wouldn't have happened if a big part of me didn't want it to occur in the first place. The Hotel had a sneaky way of not always giving its guests what they thought they wanted, but rather what they needed the most.

I got out and toweled off, determined to fight for the gift the Hotel had given me. I would fight to protect Holden and prayed it would be enough to save us both.

The bedroom door opened and shut. I froze with the towel at my feet. "Holden?" I didn't expect an answer because I sensed the presence wasn't him. I tiptoed to the bathroom door. I'd left it cracked open enough that I could glimpse a male in formal attire. I charged, forgetting about my state of undress, and had to stop short of crashing into him. "You! What are you doing here? You have a lot of nerve." Unfortunately, shouting while stark naked lacked the intimidating force I was going for. I snatched up a nearby lap quilt and covered myself, all the time maintaining an air of indignation at my uninvited guests.

Sebastian stood by my bed as David finished laying out my lost clothes—at last. I couldn't wait to be in my own clothes again.

"I'll be taking my leave," David said. "Please

accept our sincere apologies for the delay in returning your belongings. We hope you find everything in order. Good day to you, Miss."

I humphed an unintelligible thanks, and David scurried off. Sebastian hadn't moved an inch or said one word. His calm demeanor annoyed the crap out of me.

"Well?" I said. "What do you have to say?"

"You seem piqued. About what, may I ask?"

"Why yes, I am, Sebastian. Thank you for inquiring." My tone was derogatory as I threw his formal way of speaking back at him. He seemed genuinely ignorant of what was the matter. "Does lying to me ring a bell?"

"My dear Janda, I don't lie. Please forgive my lapse in recollecting what I have done to upset you. If I was in some way at fault, I assure you it wasn't intentional."

"Oh my God. You're unbelievable." I grabbed my biker clothes and headed back into the bathroom. "Don't you leave. You hear me?" I shouted at him over my shoulder.

"I wouldn't dream of it. I'll take a seat while you change," he said. "You don't have to raise your voice, either. My hearing is quite good."

I rushed to dress and dry my hair. I skipped the thong and bra, opting for a freestyle outfit that made it easier to shift. My exhaustion dissipated, and I felt like myself again in my jeans and tank top. The one item that hadn't made it back to me was my gun. I'd have to track it down before leaving the Hotel. I'd never used the weapon, but it was an added safety measure that made me more comfortable when confronting my targets when I was in my human form.

Sebastian had propped his feet up on a red velvet ottoman, his eyes closed, and was every bit the picture of royalty. His skin seemed better, less yellow, and his overall complexion wasn't as blue as when I first met him. He had fewer veins crisscrossing his arms and neck, which I figured meant he was recovering, soon to be his old, very old, self. Holden said the vamp had powerful political ties and wasn't to be messed with, but I'd given the walking dead man my blood. That alone ought to count for some level of consideration.

I took the chair next to him. He had to know I was there, yet he remained still and quiet.

"Why are you here?" The anger that had been building in me since Sebastian had marked me had subsided some, leaving me with an acute case of pissed off. It didn't seem fair that the whole time the anger had consumed me I wasn't able to lash out at Sebastian, and now that he was sitting by me I didn't have the energy to rip him a new one.

He took a deep breath, although I didn't think dead people had to breath like the rest of us, and he opened one eye to stare at me. He opened the other, sat up straighter, but he kept his legs stretched out. "I see you've calmed down some. Perhaps we can discuss matters without pointless arguing. There's much to go over before you leave."

"Why'd you mark me?"

"Why not? You were heading into a panther's hunting territory. Placing my scent on you made it so Holden's inner animal would recognize you as a friend."

"Then why not just tell me what you were doing?"

"It's never a guarantee, so giving you false confidence by assuming it would work could have cost you your life. You wouldn't have reacted in the same manner — letting your instincts guide you."

He had a valid point, but I didn't believe he needed any ego stroking. "I asked you before you bit me if doing so would bind us. You said no, yet Holden said you'd claimed me. Seems like the same thing to me. I belong to no one, so you better undo the mark."

He chuckled. "Janda, dearest, we aren't bound in the way you imagine, and the mark will wear off in time. You have nothing to fear from me."

"Yeah. You see, I'm not convinced you're telling me the whole truth. I've never known a vampire before, but I've been around my uncle my entire life and I could always tell when he was holding something back. He behaved a lot like you are now. What aren't you telling me?"

Sebastian plucked a grape from a porcelain bowl that I hadn't noticed before. I don't eat grapes, so these must have been brought for my vampire guest — the Hotel doing its thing again. Vamps might need blood to survive, but this one indulged in a variety of human foods as well. I figured it might be a way for him to keep ties to his former life as a living, breathing person, akin to a ghost caught between two worlds. Dead, but not dead. That had to suck.

It struck me that here in the Hotel, I existed in an alternate dimension separate from my normal world, and as a Lykoi I came from two different breeds. I had more in common with Sebastian than I realized — ties to two worlds and caught in between them. Yeah, it sucked.

"Very astute." He bit the grape in half, sucking on the juices before swallowing. "I know you're a Lykoi."

I tensed, waiting for the anvil to drop on my head.

"I also know why you're here — bounty huntress."

My heart skipped a few beats, and my mouth went dry. "Does Holden know?"

"Not that I am aware of." He plucked another grape, savoring the mouthful of sweetness.

He held my gaze longer than necessary, but I managed a calm I didn't feel. "Where does that leave us?"

"The same as before. You continue with everything as planned. But understand this, dear Janda, if you betray Holden, I will come after you."

The coldness of his words stung as hard as if he'd hit me.

"Fair enough."

Sebastian's threat would be a moot point because I wouldn't let anything happen to Holden. Time in this dimension was both long and short. My brief relationship with Alexander Holden felt like a lifetime of togetherness. His kiss bound me to him more effectively than if we'd been married — a prelude to a mating that both of us had waited for all our lives. I could no more live without him than without the air I breathed. If Holden died, so would I.

"I've been doing some investigating," Sebastian said, "and it's my opinion that this rogue wolf is the one you must locate. I've heard it from good authority that this wolf frequented a bar and got so inebriated he started spilling details about Myra's death. Things the killer would know and that weren't public knowledge. I'm convinced he's the killer. You find him, and we clear Holden."

"Consider it done."

Sebastian threw the grape he'd bitten across the room, where it landed expertly in the trash bin. "There's a catch, of course. My informant has told me you may know this particular wolf. He's from your pack."

"Can't be. I'd know."

"Would you?"

"Absolutely. Pack ties are strong. Murdering someone and hiding your guilt would be impossible. That's just how packs work. Everyone knows pretty much everything about, well, everyone." I was sure there was no way the rogue wolf came from my uncle's pack. If one of mine committed such a crime, he wouldn't be alive to brag about it. My uncle would kill him.

"You're a Lykoi. Can you honestly say your ties with your pack are so solid that you would sense someone's guilt?"

My knee-jerk defensiveness surfaced. "I'd know." I spoke firmly so he'd hear the ring of truth in my words. In my heart, though, I wasn't as confident.

Sebastian sighed, and the sweetness of his breath brushed my cheek as easily as if he'd been an inch away from me. Whatever he'd done created a blanket of calm around me, and I relaxed into its warmth. It was like being wrapped in a hug from a parent I'd never known. The sensation sent tears threatening to spill down my face. I coughed and rubbed at my eyes.

"I mean no disrespect," he said, "but you walk between breeds—even as a Lykoi. They say a Lykoi is a werewolf cat. Your mother was wolf, but no child of the moon—no werewolf."

"She was a shifter like the rest of my uncle's pack, but I don't see where you're going with this."

"Your bloodline won't allow you to have the same connection with a pack that you would have had if you were all wolf. The werecat in you makes that impossible, so I must disagree that you would know someone's guilt through pack ties."

"Trust me, I'd know." I may have a weak pack bond, but I'd learned how to read those I'd grown up with. Unfortunately, I had to actually be in their presence for that to work.

"Did you know werecats are either made or born, similar to your wolf kin?"

"I'd gathered as much." I wasn't sure where he was going with this topic, but I was not thrilled about the conversation. It hit way too close to home—and my insecurities.

"Holden is from a long line of werepanthers and as such has a stable nature," he said. "Those made through a bite can't always make the adjustment and go mad—killing themselves and anyone in the vicinity—in a state of extreme moon madness."

"Like my father, but he didn't hurt anyone else," I said, my temper rising. "Yes, he was a made werecat, but it wasn't moon madness that destroyed him. If his clan hadn't bullied him so much and made his life hell for choosing my mother—a wolf—he would have been fine. My mother's pack was no different. My parents were driven away by prejudice. That's what killed my father and left my mother with no will to live after giving birth to me."

"What you say has merit. Ultimately it comes back to genetic flaws that can either make us greater or destroy us. You're a werecat with wolf shifter heritage. Your pack ties are weaker than if you were pure wolf. So perhaps you don't have the same kind of ties you think you do. That's all I'm saying."

"I'd still know if a wolf from my pack was a murderer. My uncle would tell me." I couldn't keep the anger from my voice, but oddly I felt pretty darn calm.

"You've been kept on the outskirts for a reason. You're an unknown entity. More wolf or more werecat? Only time will tell."

He settled a penetrating gaze on me, as if searching for the answer, then gave up. I'd gone on that quest myself and never found what I'd been looking for, but now I didn't care. I had something more important in my life, and I didn't want to lose it.

"You're right," I said. "I've been kept at arm's length. That's why I took the contract on Holden. Escaping that life, where I'm not accepted, is all I've ever dreamed of—until Holden."

"Good. We're in agreement on one thing at least," he said in a satisfied tone.

"Did you tell him the wolf is from my pack?"

"No. If I did, Holden would never let you go. You may not have strong pack ties, but you still have them. It would make you weaker going up against one of your own, who would know how you fight and where you're most vulnerable to attacks."

"But I'd know his as well." My stubbornness came through in my tone, but Sebastian had to understand I was right. Pack ties or not, I knew how every member fought. All I needed was a name. "Who is he?" I asked.

"Asher."

"Fuck."

"You can defeat him."

"He made my childhood a nightmare, going beyond pranks to outright beating on me. My uncle turned a blind eye. Guess he figured what didn't kill me would make me stronger. The angrier I got about it, the more my uncle pushed me away."

"That couldn't have been easy, but in a way your uncle was right. He had to let you learn how to deal with prejudices because they'd follow you all your life."

"Yeah, well I learned early on to fend for myself, and I learned how to shoot." I rose. "I want my gun. Can you get it for me?"

"I'll ask, but the Hotel decides those sort of things."

"Fine. Do your best." I'd purchased the gun because it helped get the attention of my bounty targets and let them know I wasn't a push-over. I'd use it on Asher if I had the chance, assuming I was in human form. Otherwise, we'd battle it out like we'd always done. I started pacing, because that's all there was left for me to do. Patience wasn't my virtue. I wasn't sure I had any for that matter. "Holden should have been back by now with my new portal card. Where is he?"

"We're meeting him at the front entrance. I asked Selena to give me a few minutes with you. I had to be certain about your connection with Holden."

"Convinced now?"

"Yes."

I grabbed my leather jacket as we headed out the door. On the way down the hall, Sebastian paused. "One more thing."

"What now?" I hate surprises, and he was chock-full of them tonight.

"Mutther's bar is where Asher was last spotted."

I groaned and pushed past him to slam my fist on the elevator button. "I'm not getting a different portal, am I?"

"I sincerely doubt it."

We rode the elevator in silence. Sebastian did that breath thing on me again, and this time I welcomed it. I had to pull myself together so I could put up a good front for Holden's sake because he had to stay put. The doors opened, and I stepped out to the splash of the fountain echoing in the vast lobby. Selena's current dress was long and formfitting with a neckline that plunged so low it showed her navel, which held a glinting diamond stud. She stood with her arm linked with Holden's. A possessive growl escaped my throat. Selena raised a brow, Holden chuckled. I strode right up to them both and took my man by the arm. "I'm ready."

Selena relinquished him gracefully and took

Sebastian's arm instead. The four of us headed out the door, held open by David, who gave me a barely perceptible nod of approval as I swept past him. Selena's heels clicked against the stone walkway, and when we got to the end of it, she and Sebastian stopped.

"I'm afraid this is as far as we go," Sebastian said, slipping the gun into my jacket pocket. I hadn't seen where he'd gotten it from, but my guess would have been David—the best damn doorman I'd ever seen.

Selena touched Holden's arm. "The same goes for you. Any farther and you'd be in jeopardy of being pulled through the portal with Janda."

I made him step away from me, and it sent a pang of longing deep into my chest. "How will I get word to you?" I hadn't thought of the communication issue.

"I have that covered," Selena said.

She handed me the Hotel business card, and once it touched my palm an address appeared for Mutther's bar. Understanding dawned on me. Mutther was the informant, and he would be my connection with Selena. "Okay. I guess I'd better get going."

Holden reached out for my hand and pulled me into a hug that about suffocated me. "Can't breathe," I muttered into his chest. He loosened his hold just enough for me to catch my breath. I clung to him as if I'd never see him again.

Sebastian broke up the moment by clearing his throat with a loud hacking akin to a horse coughing. Who knew vamps could be so loud? It totally ruined my belief in their reputation for stealth. Vamps glided along, coming upon their victims so quietly they could get within striking distance before their prey knew what was happening. They were damn good hunters, but so was I, especially when I was on the hunt for a wolf who didn't deserve to live.

"See you on the other side," I said, kissing Holden on his stubbled cheek. God, how I loved the feel of that man.

"That's not funny," he said.

"You're just mad because you didn't think of it first." I gave him a peck on the other cheek. He growled at me, a mixture of desire and irritation that made me laugh. "I'm keeping you to your promise, Alexander Holden, so don't do anything stupid like coming through the portal before I give you the all clear."

He gave me a quick hug. "Don't keep me waiting."

"I'll try not to."

I glanced over at Sebastian and Selena. "Keep him safe." Then for Sebastian's sake I added, "Or I'll come after you."

"Fair enough," Sebastian said, chuckling at the reversal of our previous exchange.

I walked to the area where I'd stood when I had come through Mutther's portal. The white light greeted me just as before, and I turned to look back at the others. "Do you see that?" I said, but from the way Holden put his hand to his ears I understood that he couldn't hear me. I was already too far away from him and too close to the other side of the dimension.

CHAPTER EIGHT
Home Again

I focused on the biker bar and said a little prayer that it would be empty. I stumbled forward and fell flat on my face in Mutther's back hallway. Totally didn't expect that kind of an entrance.

"Nice. Very graceful," Mutther said, coming towards me.

He helped me up from the floor, and I straightened my jacket that had gotten twisted in the fall. I also checked my pocket to be sure my weapon had made it safely through the portal. It had. "Thanks," I said. "I was a ballerina in a former life. Can you tell?"

His deep laughter rang through the air. I ignored him and, with as much dignity as I could muster, walked to the bar. I *so* had to have a drink. My nerves were wound tight, and my thoughts scattered as I tried to figure out how the hell I would pull off saving Holden. I took some comfort knowing Mutther was on our side, but how much he could do and still keep his neutral status remained to be seen. The bar was empty and as spotless as the last time I was here. The main flat screen had its volume down, but the news was on and it had closed-captioning that gave the time and date. It affirmed that I'd only been gone two days, and since political debates about the upcoming elections weren't something I was interested in watching, I grabbed the remote and turned it off.

"Mind if I have a drink?"

Mutther's laughter had subsided, and he'd gone behind the bar. He produced two glasses and poured us both some Angels' Nectar. I should have sipped mine, but I wanted the burn that came with swallowing too much whiskey.

"Much better." It came out high-pitched, but it was worth it. I held my glass out to him. "Another, please."

"Since you said please."

We did this for several more rounds—four, maybe five. I'd lost count. He filled my glass again. I downed it, winced, and rubbed my tearing eyes. "Damn, that's good stuff."

"Glad you enjoyed it, because that's it for you."

"What?! I'm just getting started."

"That's what I'm afraid of." He corked the bottle and put it back on the shelf. "I'll get us some coffee."

"No need. I'm fine." The buzz hit me, and I laid my head on his well-polished bar. "I could do with some sleep, though." I mumbled into my arm, but I could tell he heard me when I looked up to see him gazing at the ceiling as if he was asking for some kind of interventional guidance from heaven on high. I had news for him—God didn't listen when it came to anything to do with me.

His gaze shifted to me. "Your bike's still in the alley," he said, "but it's four a.m. and you're not going anyplace like this. You can stay upstairs for the rest of the night. We'll talk in the morning."

He circled the bar to lead me upstairs. When I didn't move, he picked me up and carried me. I didn't protest. I had nothing left in me.

"Thanks for keeping an eye on Miss Kitty for me and making sure she stayed hidden." I loved my Harley and was glad nothing had happened to her.

"You named your bike Miss Kitty?"

"Yup." It came out muffled, because I had pressed my face against his chest to keep the dizziness at bay as well as the feeling that I was going to vomit. He probably wouldn't like it much if I threw up on him. I closed my eyes and forced the bile back down my throat.

Upstairs turned out to be Mutther's private quarters.

I tried to scope it out. The best I could do was turn my head enough to see we were in a studio apartment and that there was a bathroom off the main living area. Good to know it wouldn't be a long trek because the way my stomach was churning, I wouldn't have much time to get there. The kitchen was an alcove off to the right as we entered. It held the essentials and not much more from what I could tell. A flat screen and a sofa took up the center of the space, with a sleeping area tucked in the back corner nearest the bathroom. The decor was typical bachelor minimalist, but it had a sense of warmth that made it seem more homey than I would have expected. He placed me on his twin bed amid a cluster of pillows and rumpled blankets. I'm fairly certain I said thanks, although I couldn't swear to it. I burrowed into the mound of pillows, drew a fuzzy throw blanket over me, and fell asleep.

The next thing I knew, a crack of sunlight nailed me in the eyes and sent a shot of pain into my skull. I yanked a pillow over my head.

"Welcome home, Dorothy," Mutther said. "Time to get your sweet ass out of bed."

I peeked out from under the pillow, taking a few moments for my eyes to adjust to the lighting, then squinted up at him. "This ain't Kansas, and I'm sure no Dorothy. Besides I lost my ruby slippers." I stuck my feet out from under the blanket and wiggled my boots at him.

"Isn't that the truth?" He held out a mug of black coffee.

"Thanks." I sat up, wished I hadn't, and took the offering. I drank a quarter of it in one go. "Not too shabby."

"My specialty. That and microwave pizza."

I made a face at the mention of microwave food. "I don't know why you bother with heating up crap like that when you can hunt for your own meals." I was all about keeping my food as close to the way nature provided it as possible. Plus, I was a horrible cook.

He pulled up a chrome kitchen chair next to the bed. It was one of two that went with the yellow Formica table straight out of the sixties. "No, thanks," he said. "If I hunted all the time, then I'd be stuck with a pack. This way I have fewer rules, and I actually like frozen pizza."

"To each his own." I could relate to the pack thing. I wondered how he'd severed the ties or if he'd always been a lone wolf. He didn't say what he was, but wolf was strong in him. There was more I couldn't place, and to me he seemed to actively downplay that part of himself. Everyone had secrets.

"Feeling better?"

"Mostly," I said, rubbing the kinks in my neck and shoulders. There was a dull thumping in my ears like someone tapping on my skull from the inside. Other than that, I was fine. No more dizziness, and no more feeling like I would vomit. All good on the hangover parade. He let me take my time gaining my bearings after getting plastered the night before. I finished my coffee and put the mug on a whiskey crate that served as Mutther's nightstand. His sofa had a fleece blanket bunched in one corner where he must have used it as a makeshift pillow. "Um. Sorry to hog your bed. Didn't mean to put you out like that."

"It's fine. I've slept in worse places." He put his chair back in his dining area and refilled his mug.

"Mind if I grab a quick shower?" I had a change of clothes on the back of Miss Kitty. However I was too lazy to go get it. After a discreet whiff of my shirt I figured I'd be good for another day.

"Go for it. I'll be downstairs when you get done." He tossed me a fresh towel from the only closet in the room and left.

I was grateful for the privacy and that he didn't push the conversation about Asher that had to be dealt with soon. My encounters with Asher had never gone well in the past. He fought dirty and bullied me at every turn. He hated werecats, especially the female variety. Inwardly I shrunk from the inescapable face-off. Outwardly wasn't much better.

I tried blocking it from my mind and focused on being in the present moment. The hot water cascaded onto my head, down my backside, and ran the length of my legs to pool at my feet in the tub. The drain was slow, so the water soon surrounded my ankles. It reminded me of Holden and his waterfall. My heart ached to have him near me. I conjured an image of the two of us lathering one another with soap. My nipples stiffened at the fantasy, and I quickly rinsed and turned off the water. Frustration—that's what I got for letting my heart rule my head. If my fantasy was to become reality, then I had work to do. Mutther had somehow become part of my mission, and he was waiting downstairs.

It felt good to be cleaned up and in my old clothes —even better to have my pistol on me. While the Hotel had chosen some sexy numbers for me, which I might have to ask about keeping for future dates with a certain handsome werepanther, my biker clothes suited me best. It wasn't cold enough in the bar for my jacket, but I put it on anyway, sticking my hand in the pocket to verify the Hotel business card was still there. I drew it out, turned it over twice, shocked to see no address had been given for the portal that would take me back to the Hotel and Holden. I had a sick feeling I'd been barred from re-entering. It was more important than ever that I prove to them all that I could be trusted, or Holden would be lost to me.

I smelled pepperoni pizza as I went down the last few steps and entered the back hall. Mutther sat at the bar, a slice of microwave pizza in one hand and a beer in the other. My stomach grumbled.

He glanced up and shoved a plate of pizza in my direction. "Join me?"

"Why not?" I said, taking a seat next to him. "I'm not up for chasing down my own grub this morning."

"It's after one. It's morning some place, just not here." He poured a draft and slid it over to me.

"Yeah. You're a sharp one." I took a bite of what tasted more like cardboard than food and chased the lump down my throat with a hefty swig of beer. The bar had room-darkening shades drawn on its two windows — half windows like you'd see in a basement, yet we were above grade. The front door had been padlocked and the only other exit out the rear had a wooden plank across it bolted to the wall on both ends. Mutther didn't mess around with privacy. "Expecting company? The kind you don't want — like your mother-in-law?"

He snorted. "Good one. Not married, although I'll remember that in the future — just in case. Mothers-in-laws can be monsters. Or so I hear."

"I wouldn't know. I've heard stories. That's about it." Mutther hadn't explained the locks, and I wondered if he took such precautions all the time or if it was for my benefit. I shared his sentiments about intruders. It would be better not to have any fighting so early in my day, especially before I'd eaten. I'm cranky when I'm hungry. I finished off my slice and took another, pondering the unfamiliar concept of family ties. Holden had parents. What would his mother be like? Would they accept me? I frowned at the inevitable rejection.

"My microwave cooking that bad?"

"Not as bad as mine." I drank the rest of my beer. "Thanks for the lunch." I wiped foam from my lips and swiveled to face him. "I'm ready to get down to business."

"Good. We leave this evening."

"Okay. Maybe I should be more specific. How am I, not we, supposed to get close to Silas's nephew? I can't just walk up to Leon. And leave for where this evening?" My greater concern was finding Asher, but I had an inside connection for that task. I'd do my part with warning Leon. Then Uncle would have to tell me how to find Asher. Even if Uncle didn't know Asher's exact whereabouts, he'd give me a general area to start searching. Being familiar with Asher's scent would be a huge plus, so locating the bane of my existence wouldn't be hard once I had my lead.

"*We* are going to meet with Silas at his home this evening."

His tone brooked no argument, but I couldn't help myself from pushing his limits. "Testy, aren't you?" I stared him down — or tried to. He was pretty good at that game. Must have had a lot of practice as a kid. I know I did.

"Just telling you what's going to happen. I go, or neither of us goes. That's the deal."

"I can't help noticing you're not so neutral as you claim. What connection do you have with Silas?"

"My bar's a neutral zone. I didn't say *I* was."

"I see." Mutther was an interesting character. He liked splitting hairs. "If that's the case," I said, "then how do I know you can be trusted?"

He shrugged. "Tap into your instincts and get back to me on it."

My gut said he wouldn't betray me. That still didn't tell me where his loyalties lay in regards to werecat vs. wolf. I'd struggled with that myself over the years, but it always came down to family — those I grew up with, not the ones I'd never seen. My father's clan didn't even blink an eye at his death. That alone made me despise them. My uncle's pack was all I had in my life. I'd take the devil I knew over the one I didn't. Still, whatever Mutther's motives, he was helping me.

"You're on terms with Silas enough to go to his home. You also know Sebastian, and you're a gatekeeper for the Hotel." I plunked my mug onto the bar. "Guess I hit the jackpot because you're associated with some mighty powerful folks. But I can't say I find that comforting when I don't know how it benefits you."

He took my mug and washed it out behind the bar, the muscles around his jaw tightened, and his grip while he dried the mug had me waiting for the sound of shattering glass. He glanced at me, put the mug safely back on the shelf, and tossed the towel on the countertop.

"I lost someone close to me a long way back. Thought I'd go mad with grief. Silas found me half-starved and gutter drunk. He took pity and sent word to Nick, who gave me a temporary home. It didn't last. Couldn't, really. I had too much hate in me. Made it impossible for pack bonds to form, and I didn't want the ties. That's when Sebastian came into the picture and showed me how I could live as an outlier. It worked, and here I am today, paying it forward."

I itched to know more because my gut also said he hadn't told me the whole story, but some things are best left buried. What Mutther revealed was enough. He wanted justice for Myra, whose death reminded him of his own loss, so he'd do what he could to get the right killer. On this we were of the same mind.

"I assume you know the score," I said. "I meet with Silas so I can get close to his nephew without raising too many questions. Once I deliver Holden's warning to Leon, I'm free to pursue the other aspect of this case—finding Asher. Without more detailed information on who might be behind an attempted takeover, Leon will have to be extra careful, but if I can get to Asher, we may be able to figure out who's responsible."

Mutther pushed his drink aside. "We also don't know how deep this plot goes, assuming it *is* a plan to oust Silas and his successors. There's still the possibility it's simply a rogue wolf preying on a weaker target. I can't do much to help you with Asher other than giving you safe passage through Silas's territory and introducing you to the wolf pack whose land borders Silas's. You sort of met the pack leader when you first arrived."

"Nick? He's the pack leader here?"

Mutther nodded, his amusement evident in his eyes. "Just don't play poker with him, and you'll be fine."

I sighed. "Why is my life so messy? Seriously? Biker Nick?" I laid my hands on the counter and leaned inward, as if about to impart a great secret. "Ever hear of the saying 'one card short of a full deck'? That's your biker friend. He had to have suffered a head injury because you can't be as thick as he came off the other night. Or booze could have destroyed his brain cells. Either way, I don't want to deal with him."

Mutther crooked a finger, signaling me to come even closer. His turn to share a nugget of wisdom. He lowered his voice just above a whisper. "You won't get far if you don't get on his good side."

"Says you." I sat with my arms folded across my chest.

His voice returned to normal. "Yep, so you better take my advice. He's not the brightest, but he's fair. He's also not as stupid as he seemed the other night. He keeps his pack in line and is fuming about Asher coming into the bar and implying he killed Myra. He's a slick bastard. Came just short of admitting he did it, so we couldn't turn him in. We can't do shit to him, and the gloating bastard knows it."

"Guess you're stuck with pack rules regardless of being an outsider. Welcome to my world."

"Point taken."

"If everyone thinks Asher did it, then why didn't Silas cancel my contract? He must know Holden is innocent."

"You think he's innocent—and maybe he is, but maybe he isn't. That's for you to decide once you learn the truth. In the meantime, the contract stands."

"What does Silas believe?"

"It's complicated, and I'm not sure I could even explain it well enough."

"Try me."

A swath of sunlight poked through the gap between the shade and the windowsill, casting its glow on the hardwood floor and highlighting the deep scratches that marred the surface. Mutther's bar had seen its share of scuffles, presumably before it became a neutral zone.

He came back around the counter and took up his seat once more. "For starters, Silas can't afford to go to war with the wolves. Nick denies any involvement, but he's still accountable for keeping track of wolves passing through. Silas partly blames Nick for allowing Asher to be here. Silas also isn't convinced Holden didn't hire Asher. So even though Holden may not have laid hands on Myra, he could still be the one who got Asher to do the dirty work. I've talked to Silas about other possibilities, such as Asher being hired by a rival clan—the theory Holden favors. Of course, we could be wrong about all of it and Asher might have done it for his own reasons."

"Like his hatred for female werecats," I added.

"Myra could have been in the wrong place at the wrong time—a murder of opportunity. Could be you bring that out in Asher since he's been forced to live with a part-werecat his whole life."

"Are you saying I might be responsible for Myra's death?"

"Of course not. Asher is the one to be held accountable for his actions, no one else. Psychologically his killing could stem from his irrational hatred of you, and Myra might only be the first of many more to come if he isn't stopped."

Mutther's diagnosis of Asher's mental makeup

made a lot of sense, but it bothered me to think I could be the root of all this trouble. "He's not the only one who doesn't want harmony and equality among the wolf and cat communities. He's just the vocal one. According to him, I'm an abomination."

"There are too many ways this could have gone down," Mutther said, his tone rising with his obvious frustration. "That's why Silas hired you to reach Holden — to find out the truth by bringing Holden back — except you're out here and Holden is still at the Hotel. Then there's the fact you have ties to Asher. See the rub? Trust is in short supply."

"That doesn't explain why Asher's still alive."

"Politics comes in all forms. Asher can't be killed by one of us unless he attacks us directly. If we can prove he's the murderer, then we could turn him over to human authorities. However, there are quite a few who would rather he didn't make it through the booking process."

"So that's where I come in? I'm in his pack. I can go after him without fear of starting a bloodbath."

"I see you get the general idea."

"Great. Kill Asher. Face my Uncle Damon." I got up from my seat and strode over to yank the shade down completely and block out the sun that was now irritating the shit out of me. "Just another day in paradise," I said. We couldn't move forward with our plan until evening, which was too far off to ease my need for action. "All we've done is talk this thing to death. I have to get out of here and go for a run, or I'll end up doing something stupid."

"Like tracking Asher before warning Leon," Mutther said.

I shoved a chair into a table. "Or worse." The business card was warm to my touch. I wanted to be with Holden, and if I couldn't unleash some of my pent up frustration I'd find a way to get back into the Hotel.

Mutther made a quick call, keeping his voice so low I couldn't make out the words. "Okay," he said. "We have permission to go hunting."

He unbolted the back door and slid the plank free, giving me access to the alley. Beyond it trees rose to mark the edge of the woods. We went outside, and after Mutther did a quick check of the surroundings, he started to shift. I pulled off my jacket, being careful to keep the gun tucked inside it, and hid everything behind a bin by the door. I kicked off my boots to join him, delighted in tasting the freedom of being Lykoi.

CHAPTER NINE
Old Enemies

I padded softly through the underbrush and found a spot to wait. The mustiness of leaves beneath me lifted my spirits. Mutther held a position far enough to my rear so as not to disrupt my hunting. We'd started out running through the woods until my restlessness eased and I could focus on food. I wasn't overly hungry, so small game would suffice. I had a particular fondness for rabbit. It seemed my inclinations leaned more to the wolf side than werecat when it came to hunting. Whether that was nature or nurture I couldn't say for sure. I'd never been taught anything other than the wolf way.

A whiff of ammonia put me on alert. A buck rabbit marked his territory, and I set my sights on him. I glanced back at Mutther, who crouched in his wolf form and kept low to the ground, well away from my target area. He was here solely as my companion—or more likely just to keep me from getting into trouble. I'm sure he had to pull a few strings to allow me to run as Lykoi.

The rabbit hopped off between two trees and froze just short of the underbrush. I prepared to leap then froze as well.

A large gray wolf emerged from the opposite direction and lunged at the rabbit, tearing its head off and ripping the torso into shreds. The wolf's scent reached me, but I'd recognize Asher without it. He continued to shred the rabbit, never once swallowing a bit—a wasteful use of life. Mutther crept forward a few inches. I narrowed my gaze at him in warning. This was my fight.

I rose to all fours and pushed my way through the shrubbery. Asher whirled around, blood dripping from his muzzle. He was larger than me by at least sixty pounds—and I weighed in at one-twenty. He'd always outweighed me, but I was faster. I approached then stopped just out of his striking range and cursed the bad luck that seemed to constantly follow me. My gun was back at the bar, and I was Lykoi. I didn't want to be the first to shift back, and he didn't seem to take the hint. He placed a protective paw over his kill, claiming it as his, which was nothing new. If he was in a generous mood, he might leave me a few bones to pick over, but I wasn't interested in his leftovers. I remained motionless, letting my body language do the communicating. He knew me well enough to understand I was gearing for a fight.

The idiot grinned. It'd been years since we'd gotten into a brawl, mainly because I'd stayed clear of him, but also because Uncle had finally banned the two of us from fighting. I got up and pawed at the ground. Asher snarled but didn't shift back to human. I had to get him to change or we might never discover who was responsible for Myra's death.

I moved farther back and began my

transformation. Asher kept his ground. Only when I'd completed the change did he venture to do the same.

"Janda. What brings you to these parts?" Asher took a casual step forward.

I didn't budge. "Work."

"Really? How interesting. Anyone I know?"

"I'd say so." I analyzed his features and the way he swung his arms as he walked closer. I could tell he was sizing me up as well—our usual posturing.

We were both naked—nothing we hadn't seen before and nothing that mattered to either of us. By now we should have been pulling out our clothes that'd been tucked away in a safe retrieval spot. I hadn't thought to bring mine and if he had any, he wasn't bothering to get them.

"Have you found this person yet?"

"Yes, I have. Thanks." I sidestepped, making a half circle around him. "Why'd you do it?"

He mirrored my movements, keeping pace with me. "Do what?"

"The woman. Why'd you kill her?"

Deep laughter filled the distance between us. "She wasn't a woman. She was an abomination. Like you."

I growled at him—not as effective in my human form, but he got the point.

He took a huge leap in the air, twisting his body and becoming wolf again. I was ready. A rustling in the trees meant Mutther was also about to attack. I could use the backup, but for this single moment Asher was all mine. I shifted to Lykoi seconds before impact. Air left my lungs in a whoosh that had me gasping. I rolled and sprang up, still wheezing. I took a deep breath, and with the speed I'm known for slammed into him. He lost his balance, falling on his side. I bit into the soft spot on his neck and sunk my teeth deeper, aiming for the jugular. He yelped. I was elated to have hurt him, although I'd missed my intended mark.

The sentiment was lost in an instant. He threw me off and landed on top of me, pressing hard on my windpipe with his massive paw. Darkness filled my peripheral vision, yet the black blur that flew across my body and into Asher was one I recognized instantly—Holden.

Gray and black intertwined into an indistinguishable mass of wolf and panther fur. I wanted to join the fray but feared getting in Holden's way. I paced on the edge of the fighting, searching for an opportunity to strike. A high-pitched yowl pierced the air. Splatters of red flew in my direction, covering my sparse fur. I halted, lifted my paw to my mouth, and licked the blood. It was Asher's. I'd memorized the taste of it from years ago when I'd given him a bloody nose. Relief surged through me, and I resumed my pacing.

Holden didn't let up on the attack until Asher no longer moved. Wolf became man in death with Asher's bloody corpse sprawled at my feet. I gave it a perfunctory sniff then looked over at Holden. I'm not a pretty creature in my Lykoi appearance, and having Holden see me as I truly am made me ashamed. With Mutther it didn't matter what he thought of me, so I didn't care that he'd seen my shifter form. Holden was a different story, yet I didn't run and hide like I wanted to, not if he might need my help. I walked around him, searching for injuries, brushing against him as I went. He didn't shy away, but he didn't greet me with unbounded joy either.

Mutther stepped from the trees in his human form fully dressed, of course. He held my spare clothes bundled in his arms. He must have stashed them somewhere in preparation for our appointment this evening with Silas. Such meetings normally would end with a group hunt as a sign of acceptance. What would happen now that Asher was dead? Fear constricted my throat, and I hastened to turn back into my human shape.

"I'll say it was me." My voice sounded gravelly from the bruised windpipe, and my side ached with what was probably a cracked rib. I took the clothes from Mutther, babbling while I dressed. "My uncle won't be surprised when I tell him. We've been at the brink of this for ages."

"No." Holden practically growled his objection. He'd shifted as well and stood in all his naked glory.

"It has to be me," I said. I would have begged if I thought it would change anything. I could tell Holden's pride wouldn't allow me to take the blame.

"No. I'll deal with it."

"You shouldn't even be here. I had this." I wanted to hit him for being so stupid as to leave the safety of the Hotel.

"It didn't look to me like you had it. He had you. By the throat. Choking the life out of you."

"He wouldn't have killed me or he would have had to face my uncle. He liked teaching me the lessons of life, as he called them. That's all." I wouldn't admit it, but Asher had gone over the line this time and would have snuffed out my last breath if Holden hadn't intervened. I'd thought Mutther would come to my aid, not Holden.

"And where were you in all this?" I gave Mutther a scathing look.

"Right where you left me, with strict orders from higher authorities to not touch Asher. I wouldn't have let him kill you but Holden came out of nowhere and plunged headlong into the fight." Mutther handed him a pair of jeans. "These will have to suffice. And why did you come?"

"Thanks." Holden pulled them on. "Selena let it slip that you were going after an old rival. It was driving me crazy thinking about you out here facing Asher. I couldn't take it any longer. I bribed Selena to give me access to your portal." He went back to Asher. "Not how I wanted this to go down." He let out a tired breath.

I hurriedly put on my clothes, then Mutther and I joined Holden. He held my hand, lending his quiet support and giving me a moment to face my past. I stared down at the man who'd made my life a living nightmare and felt nothing at his demise.

"My phone's in my jacket at the bar. I'll give Uncle a call. He'll send someone to take Asher home. Then you and I will have a serious discussion about our future."

Holden stiffened, pulling me close. Mutther took a position on my other side. I sensed the tension in the air. We weren't alone. Eyes peered at us from the woods, both human and animal.

A man strode barefoot towards us. He wore khaki

pants and no shirt. His browned skin was more from the sun than natural like Holden's. He wore his hair pulled back in a short ponytail and reminded me of a smaller version of Silas Vang—the oriental heritage evident in the shape of the face and eyes.

"Alex. Mutther," he said, his greeting terse. He stopped in front of my protectors then glanced over at the body and back to Holden. "I see you found Asher."

"You could say that," Holden said.

"How did you know where to find us, Leon?" Mutther said.

I was sure he mentioned Leon by name to let me know who we were facing. The family resemblance was strong in the Vang family. The pictures I'd seen of Myra spoke of the same genetic traits. Mutther kept the space between us to a minimum, so I was firmly wedged between him and Holden. Leon met my gaze. I held it. This was the man I was sent to warn. Holden could pass that warning along if he was given the chance. Neither he nor Mutther relaxed their stance, indicating our fate hadn't been decided yet.

Leon turned to Mutther, never acknowledging me beyond his brief scrutiny.

"Silas said he gave you permission to hunt. He didn't tell me you had company or that what you were hunting was Asher."

Mutther bristled at the implication. "It came as quite a surprise to us, too." He pointed at the blood still evident around Asher's mouth. "We were after the same dinner. He got to it first and didn't take kindly to being interrupted."

"Who killed him?"

"I did," Holden said. "He admitted to murdering Myra. Mutther heard him."

Holden took half a step forward, staying between Leon and me. He still had my hand and gave it a tight squeeze, warning me to remain quiet. I'm not prone to keeping my mouth shut, but didn't want to make things worse by saying the wrong thing.

Leon tensed.

"That's right," Mutther said. "Unfortunately, he attacked before we could get any other information from him."

"Very unfortunate," Leon said. He held his hand in the air and motioned for those with him to come forward. "I'm sorry, Holden. I have to take you in."

Holden's muscles went taught. He pulled me behind him, never letting go of my hand.

"Don't make this hard on us—or her." Leon's threat was clear.

"Just me." Holden released his grip.

"Of course. Mutther and the girl are free to go."

Leon stepped aside so two of his men could take custody of Holden. Asher's body was carted off, and Holden followed resolutely behind them, leaving me with Mutther. Leon started after his men.

"What will happen to him?" I had to speak up. Mutther had become a mute, while half my soul was being ripped away from me.

Leon halted in his tracks. "He'll have a clan trial. Nothing that need concern you." Leon joined his men, marching Holden out of sight.

Mutther grabbed my wrist, holding me in place. "Wait," he whispered. "We'll come at this a different way."

My chest tightened. "What way? They took Holden. Do you really think he'll get a fair trial?"

"Silas is a good leader. Holden will get the fairest trial possible."

"Leon wants Holden dead. You can't tell me you didn't see the way he itched to get revenge. Why didn't you tell him about the rival clan threat? Why didn't you stop them from taking Holden?" I fumed helplessly.

"Come on. It'll be okay," he said, his voice consoling in low, soothing tones.

He gave me a gentle tug, guiding me back the way we'd come. I followed blindly, not feeling the branches whipping my arms and legs. I'd lost the gift the Hotel had given me. I'd lost Holden.

CHAPTER TEN
Trial of the Heart

Once we were back in the bar, I called Uncle Damon and left a voicemail. Although not the best way to break the news of Asher's death, it was all I could do. I'd wanted to speak to Uncle directly, feel him out about his emotional state and what I would be facing on my return. I didn't have time to wait for his call and see what would happen to me. It wouldn't matter if I couldn't save Holden.

While I attempted to reach my uncle, Mutther placed a few calls himself. From his sour expression I gathered he hadn't had much success either.

"What now, Einstein?"

He shook his head and handed me a glass of whiskey. "We wait."

"Not a chance." I took the drink and munched a handful of peanuts he kept on the bar without registering what I was doing. My mind was elsewhere, and I was feverishly planning my next move—a novelty for me.

"I can't do anything without further word from the higher ups, or—"

"Risk starting a war," I said, filling in the blanks. "Same old tune, different station."

He threw up his hands in disgust. "You don't know about politics. If I make a move without permission, the repercussions could be devastating."

"You have more rules than you think, and I don't care about repercussions. I care about Alexander Holden."

"My point exactly."

His phone rang, cutting off anything else he was about to say to me. Mutther's ties ran deeper than he pretended. Whether or not those ties would keep me from my own pursuits was something I had to consider. It might be time for me to ditch Mutther and go it alone.

"Yes," he said into the phone. He listened to whoever spoke on the other end, nodding in my direction and giving me the thumbs up.

I tried several times in the past hour to discover who he was contacting, but he wouldn't say. I could tell it was a male voice, but that was it. My hearing was acute, but wolves knew how to keep their conversations relatively private when they wanted to, unless they were drunk like biker Nick had been when he practically woke the dead with his antics three nights ago.

I stared into space while Mutther droned on. Three days had changed everything for me. I didn't have a life before Holden, and once I'd gotten a taste of what happiness could be, I'd do anything to keep it.

A text popped up on my phone—a message from Silas. *Will get bank check in morning. Good job luring Holden out of hiding. Trial tonight. Attend and see clan justice.*

I sat there, dazed and dumbfounded. I would have cut off my arm rather than hurt Holden. Once Silas told him why I went to the Hotel, I doubted Holden would believe how I felt. Mutther's droning ceased. He touched my hand. I jumped.

"Sorry," he said. "My contact suggested we find where Asher was hiding out and see if we can discover any evidence linking him to whoever might have a vested interest in seeing Silas's clan fall apart."

"Huh?" I'd missed about half of what he'd said. Guilt was eating my insides and making it impossible to focus.

"Never mind." He cleared away my drink and the nuts. "You need to snap out of it. We have work to do."

I blinked away tears building at the corners of my eyes. "I've signed his death warrant."

"Not yet you haven't."

"The trial's tonight at sundown."

"Damn."

"I am damned. Cursed to hell, which is what I deserve."

"Where's the feisty Lykoi that charged into my bar the other night?"

I glanced at him, still fighting with my inner demons and losing miserably. "She's dead without him."

Mutther slapped my face. My cheek burned.

"What the fuck?!"

He grinned. "There she is."

"You asshole." But he was right. I'd wasted time feeling sorry for myself. No matter what the outcome tonight, I wouldn't sit here passively and let it happen. "You made your point. Now what do we do?"

"We work backwards."

"Backwards?"

"Yeah. Forwards is when you track your prey by locating their trail to find out where they are. We're going to do the opposite — starting where we found him and going backwards to discover where he's been. And hope it works."

I understood where he was headed with this, which meant I'd already spent too much time around Mutther. His logic was rubbing off on me. "Then it's off to the woods and where Asher was killed." A few hours were all I had left to prove Holden's innocence.

We found blood-soaked leaves smelling of rust and mold in the spot Asher died. There were so many scents littering the area it was impossible to pinpoint Asher's. I muttered my discontent, walking in an outward spiral from where the body had lain. The farther out I went, the fainter Asher's trail became, mainly because the blood splatters had ended.

"It's NOT working." I pounded my fist against a pine tree, sending a cascade of needles showering onto me and inundating me with the smell of fresh pine. *Great.*

Mutther stood where I had been while hunting the rabbit. "You were here. Asher came from that direction."

He pointed to a stand of trees off to the left of me. I went to where he indicated and surveyed the ground. No blood. A lot of crushed plant life and footprints galore. "Maybe I should shift. My senses are so much better as Lykoi, but communicating with you would suck, and .I wouldn't be able to keep calling Uncle Damon, so never mind. I'll do it this way." I got on all fours and crawled along the ground, my head tucked low and making a sweeping movement from side to side. Sifting through the scents from the myriad of humans and animals that had trampled the ground took time. The sun moved closer to the horizon. The minutes passed while I searched in vain for Asher's trail, and Holden's future became bleaker.

I got up, stretched, and pulled out my phone. Uncle didn't answer. I left another voicemail. I glared at Mutther, my frustration rising out of control. "Where the hell is he? Uncle should be able to help. He had to know Asher was here. Maybe even know where Asher held up."

"He didn't stay in town. I checked. No one saw him other than when he came to my bar. He had to have been living out here someplace."

I opened my arms wide. "Do you see how much territory we have to cover? It's impossible." I plunked down on a fallen log. "I don't get why Asher would stick around after killing Myra. It doesn't add up." I glanced over at Mutther. "We're missing something."

He came to sit next to me and tipped his head back to look up at the sky.

"That's the third time I've seen you do that. Are you praying? If you are, don't bother."

He chuckled. "No. I get knots in my neck when I'm tense. I'm just trying to loosen the muscles, but

I'm not averse to tossing in a few prayers."

"Whatever makes you feel better." My mind was stuck on why Asher hadn't left the area. "Seriously, though, why would Asher stay?"

"Some killers like seeing the reaction their deed has on others. Gives them an emotional high of sorts."

I could see Asher getting off on people's pain and heartache. He'd loved watching me suffer growing up. He was a sadistic beast. Yet as I thought back on our childhood, Asher didn't generally cause grief for grief's sake, he had ulterior motives—like trying to get me to run away or make my uncle mad at me. Most of the time he also had a sidekick—until the other guys got fed up with getting into trouble over a girl who wasn't worth their notice and Uncle laid down the law.

"He had an accomplice." As soon as I said it, I knew it was true.

"So Holden could have been involved."

"NO!" I smacked Mutther. "No way in hell would he stoop so low as to murder his future wife." My experience with Holden at the Hotel was brief in this dimension—how long in the other was anyone's guess—yet I knew Holden's character was an honorable one.

"I'm not saying he's behind this, but Silas won't be able to rule him out either." He took his phone from his pocket. "Time to call in backup."

I rubbed pine sap from my palm by gathering a handful of dirt. It felt good to have a connection with the land. I'd always dreamed of earning enough money to build a cabin in the woods, away from pack rules and the side-glances I'd endured living as a half-breed among wolves. In the seclusion of nature, I had freedom. However, the price for it had become too steep. Holden may never forgive me for my part in his capture, and if he survived his ordeal, I wouldn't blame him for never wanting to see me again. As long as he lived I could let him go, despite how it would tear me apart. If he didn't make it, I'd die with him.

A twig snapped. I stood, ready for an attack, on the brink of shifting. Mutther gripped my shoulder.

"It's fine. Backup's here. Come on out, Nick."

Biker Nick came up to us. He appeared exactly as he had the other night, right down to his well-worn boots.

"You got here fast," Mutther said, reaching out to shake Nick's hand and clap his back.

"We were in the area. Doing our own search. Figured the more the merrier."

Nick's three companions took up position behind him, forming a wall of human flesh. It was an impressive sight. They glanced at me but said nothing. Nick would decide how to treat me, and the others would follow his lead. This was protocol, not prejudice. I'd do this by the book and let Mutther handle the introductions.

"This is Janda. She's new to these parts and has a close connection to those we support."

I waited for Nick to make the first move. Mutther had done what he could. The rest was up to the one-percenter looming over me. He was freakishly tall— close to seven feet—and as broad-chested as a lumberjack. He inhaled a long draw of breath, his head tilted slightly upward.

"Sebastian's mark," he said. "Good enough for me."

Well damn. I'd thought it would have worn off by now, especially after getting Asher's blood on me. Granted, I'd washed when I'd returned to the bar, but Asher's stink had to still be in my hair. Sebastian's mark must be a lot stronger than I'd imagined.

"Thanks," I said, a bit taken back by the magnitude of Sebastian's clout. The dead man walking was a popular guy.

"We can use the help," Mutther said. "It's too contaminated here for us to make much headway, and we're about out of time." He produced a piece of Asher's bloodied clothing and passed it around to the others.

Nick nodded to his men, and they split off to comb the woods. Nick stayed behind. "What else do you need from us?"

"There's an Elders' meeting about to take place. I've been asked to join them."

"Let them know I've done my part. I'll give a full report later."

"I'll pass that along. If there's any hint of a rival clan trying to take over Silas's territory, we'll find out tonight. I can't miss this chance, but Janda's going to need an escort to the trial." Mutther hesitated. "You know I wouldn't ask if I had any other choice."

Nick grumbled his annoyance. "Will they allow it?"

"Silas wants Janda present. He seems to feel it's important for her to understand clan dynamics—get to know the other side of her heritage. I'll let him know you'll be bringing her."

"Why can't I go alone?" My irritation at feeling like I was invisible came through in my tone. I was a person, not an object, and I had a mind of my own. This would be my first time within the inner workings of a clan, and I was ready to see what my father's people were like. I also wanted to know more about the Elders. I'd heard of them growing up, but Uncle kept mum about anything to do with them. "And don't say it's because of protocol."

Nick glanced at Mutther, who pursed his lips.

"Then let's just say it's propriety." Mutther said.

I shook my head in disgust. "Semantics. Fine. I'll have to reach Silas because he never told me where to go."

"I know where," Nick said. "Trials are held at neutral combat grounds. Gives fighters more space, and reduces the risk of bystander injuries. It also allows for others to be witnesses without worrying about territorial boundaries."

"Fighting!" I felt myself flush with anger. Mutther stepped away from me while Nick looked amused.

"The accused, under certain circumstances, will have the right to trial by combat. A fight to the death. Surely your pack has something like this?" Mutther said.

"I suppose, but I've never been to one." I had to search my memory for instances of pack trials and realized I'd never been allowed to go near any of Uncle's official gatherings. He kept me out of sight and always had one of the women stay with me. Fresh waves of pain ran over me. I pushed them down and met the men's gazes. "If anything happens to Holden, they'll have to answer to me."

Nick actually chuckled. It sounded like a grizzly bear with gas issues.

"I'm calling Uncle again." It went straight to voicemail. "What the hell is he doing?" I would have tossed the phone into the tree line if it wasn't the only thing keeping me tethered to what was happening with Holden. I'd already discovered Holden's phone had been turned off and probably confiscated. I hadn't heard any more news from Silas either, but I wasn't above calling him. I just didn't want to do it until I had some good news. Now that didn't look likely to happen.

"We have roughly an hour left," Mutther said. "I wish I could be more optimistic, but I think the only thing that might help is you."

"Me?" If I could have helped already, I would have, and not being able to made me want to shout at the world about how unfair life was and how the justice system sucked.

"I've been reasoning this through, and you might be Holden's one shot at making them think twice about his guilt. You've been with him these past few days. You can be a character witness. Testify on his behalf."

"I'm a half-breed. A nobody. Who would care what I had to say?" My old rant surfaced, and it was bitter tasting.

"That's where you're wrong. You're the perfect person. You were hired by Silas but discovered first-hand that Holden might be innocent. He sent you back to warn Leon. You also can tell them about Asher—how he treated you and his hatred for werecat women."

I mulled over what Mutther said. It was all true. I'd have to disclose my motives for going to the Hotel, putting myself out there for all to see and judge me by. Holden would despise me, but any shot at saving him was worth losing the love of my life.

"Will Silas let me testify?"

"If you declare yourself as primary witness for the defense, they have to let you speak," Nick said. "That much is standard procedure among packs and clans alike."

I glanced at the sunlight turning orange as it filtered through the trees. "Show me the way."

Mutther gave me a peck on the cheek, surprising me with his gesture.

"No matter how this plays out I want you to know I appreciate what you've done for me—and for Holden. You're a good guy." I wrapped my arms around him in a quick embrace. "Thanks. I owe you."

"You owe me nothing," he said. "What you're about to do will pave the way for others like you to follow. Believe you're equal and they will have to treat you as such. It just takes time." He shoved me gently towards Nick. "Now show them what you're made of, Janda Gray."

CHAPTER ELEVEN
Justice for All

I unveiled Miss Kitty and pushed her from the alley.

"Sweet ride," Nick said.

"She's my baby." A real mother couldn't be prouder than I was of Miss Kitty.

I ran my hand over the handlebars and checked to be sure nothing had happened to her while I was at the Hotel. She was perfect. Mutther had been true to his word and had taken good care of my Harley. I slid my arms into my jacket and put on my helmet. I might not be totally human, but I still got hurt the same—and road rash was a bitch, especially on the face. I learned the hard way, but I did learn.

"It's about ninety miles from here," Nick said.

"Ninety? We'll never make it." It'd taken us ten minutes to jog back from where we left Nick's men scouring the woods plus the time it took to grab my gear.

Nick got on his bike and revved the engine. "Follow my lead, and the cops won't stop us. Keep to the limits in town, and once we're on open road we can let 'em loose."

"Fine by me." I started Miss Kitty, and she

hummed a low purr, waiting for the all clear.

"Mind the curves. Some of them can be sharp, and we don't have time to scrape you off the road."

"Don't worry about me. I have this."

Nick grinned, showing a gap between his front teeth. "I bet you do, darlin'. I bet you do."

I was beginning to like the Neanderthal. We drove down the street, past people out for a leisurely autumn stroll in this sleepy-eyed place tucked in the hollows of the Catskill Mountains. A few cars motored by in the other direction, nothing to slow our progress, and soon we hit the outskirts of town, heading back the way I'd come when I first got to town. I gave Miss Kitty some throttle just as Nick did the same with his bike, staying off the thruway so we wouldn't attract attention with how fast we were going. We tore through the countryside, winding around the base of hills, and the sun seemed to stand still to watch us. If only I could stop it from setting.

Darkness gathered around us, and I had to turn on my lights. My heart raced along with my bike, faster and faster with every curve we took. It wasn't long until Nick slowed to near speed limit and I was forced to do the same. The way had become more difficult to follow in the dark even though I was somewhat familiar with the road we took—back to my home and Sleepy Hollow. Still, I eased off the throttle. We'd be no good to Holden if we crashed. I alternated between grinding my teeth and cursing out loud. Nick's voice drifted back to me on the air current.

"Almost there."

One curve down, then another. I must have

misunderstood what Nick had tried to tell me because we drove on. I was in a nightmare where you run down the hall to reach the door but the hallway kept getting longer and the door farther away.

Nick honked his horn and flashed his lights. I slowed, pulling up close to him. "Please tell me we're here," I said, raising my voice to be heard.

He nodded and signaled for me to get off onto a side road. His light as he turned illuminated a sign—Sleepy Hollow Forest.

Of course, I was back in Westchester County—practically in my own backyard—but in an area I hadn't spent much time in because Uncle had declared it off-limits to me. We passed torches posted along the dirt road that sent flickers of light dancing among the trees and reminded me of the chandeliers at the Hotel—and of Holden in his Green Room jungle.

Nick had dropped his speed to an agonizing crawl, and I followed suit. Beyond the torches, shadowed forms emerged, lining our path and watching our progress. The sentinels drew closer to us, walking in small groups until they formed an odd kind of parade behind our bikes, yet they never attempted to stop us or speak to us. I found the whole thing rather intimidating, which I'm sure was the intent.

Up ahead was a parking area jammed with motorcycles of every variety, and beyond it was a large clearing with a fire pit that sent flames leaping into the air. We parked as close to the road as possible, just in case we had to do a fast retreat. I turned off Miss Kitty and placed my helmet on the seat. Nick came up behind me to cover the rear and make sure no one could get too close. It was a nice gesture but a useless one if this gathering turned into an angry mob. I didn't say anything to Nick about it — probably he already knew — yet we had to act like we belonged here to maintain solidarity and show them we were a force to be reckoned with. And we were. We'd take down as many of them as we could if it came to it. I hoped it wouldn't.

Silas, an older variation of Leon, left his spot near the head of the semi-circle encompassing the fire and approached us. The group to our rear paused, waiting for instructions from their leader. He waved them off, and they dispersed to take up seats in the clearing. There were too many people and not enough seats — standing room only.

"Janda! I'm so glad you made it." Silas wrapped an arm around my shoulder then nodded to Nick, who remained protectively close to my side.

Silas lead us to a makeshift bench — a tree that'd been cut down and propped on cinderblocks at each end. It'd been set up on one side of the fire pit with a similar arrangement on the opposite side. The occupants vacated their seats at our approach. We were being given a place of honor, a front-row view of the proceedings.

I stifled a gasp at the sight of Holden shackled in iron chains that had been pinioned to the ground on either side of the wooden stool he sat upon. The firelight cast shadows over him, making the bruise on his cheek seem darker and the cut on his lip deeper. Encased in the fire's glow, his back ramrod straight, he stared at Silas and only gave me a slight nod to let me know he was okay. I doubted anyone else had caught the communication, and I assumed it meant I was to maintain the pretense of bounty huntress — the person responsible for bringing Holden to justice.

Nick sat on my right, Silas to my left. Neither acknowledged the other. Once we were seated, Leon got up from a bench opposite us and came forward.

"As I was about to say before the interruption," Leon glowered at me, "the facts presented earlier clearly demonstrate motive and opportunity. Myra, my darling baby sister, was set up from the start by this man." He sidestepped and pointed an accusatory finger at Holden. "She had accepted him as her future spouse but was humiliated by his very vocal and public rejection, as can be attested to by any number of witnesses present here today."

A low rumble of affirmation spread through the crowd.

"Yes, yes," Silas said. "This is all public knowledge. Myra was mistreated by Holden, no disputing it. What we must prove here this evening is if that action induced the accused to commit murder." He stared at Leon. "What proof can you present to that fact?"

Leon scowled for a moment and then seemed to remember himself and quickly backtracked, giving his uncle a thin smile. He produced a plastic bag containing a woman's shirt that he passed to Silas, who opened it and smelled the interior before handing it to a man on his left. I would have liked to have had a chance to examine the contents, because I was almost certain the scent that reached me was Asher's with a hint of Holden's as well.

Leon had to link the two men to the crime and to each other. Asher's confession didn't seem to be the issue. His connection to Holden was the real question. Had Holden hired Asher? I couldn't bring myself to believe it.

"As a matter of fact, I can prove beyond a shadow of a doubt that Holden and Asher plotted together to kill my sister." He produced a snapshot that he gave to Silas.

My breath caught at the sight of Holden and Asher outside Mutther's bar. They seemed to be talking. This was pretty damning information. Leon had just connected the men to one another, and Asher's guilt had already been established with his confession. Holden seemed to be guilty by association, but just what that association was remained a mystery. Snapshots don't speak. They only take a moment in time, out of context, and put it out for all to see. To me the photo didn't prove crap. The crowd around me had a different opinion. Their murmurs grew into a chant of 'justice for Myra'.

"Myra's shirt has both men's scent, the photograph shows them together, we have Holden's public rejection of Myra, and may I remind the court of his angry response when designated as the future clan leader? Holden was found at the scene of the crime. What more do we need to prove?"

"Kill him!"

I searched for who had shouted, but it was impossible to tell. The crowd grew noisy, and Silas had to yell over them.

"Enough!" Silas rose to face his people.

Leon had a smug expression as he soaked in the glory of his victory.

I couldn't take it any longer. I jumped up from my seat. "It's not true!" I shouted at the top of my lungs.

Holden shook his head vehemently at me. "No, Janda. Stay out of this." His panic-filled voice brought the ruckus to a halt. All eyes were on him.

Silas stepped nearer to him. "Have you decided to break your silence and defend yourself? Or confess?"

Holden relaxed his taut grip on the chains that he'd stretched to their limits in an attempt to reach me. I was certain if he'd managed to pull free, he'd be torn apart by the frenzied group he called his clan and he'd let it happen.

"You've made your decision. I have nothing to say." Holden gave me a sharp look of disapproval before resuming his former stance.

Silas sighed at Holden then looked over at me. "You disagree with Leon?"

"Yes." Up until this point I'd been actively ignored, the standard reaction to my presence that I'd grown accustomed to over the years. Normally I'd back off, retreat within myself, and pretend it didn't matter. I remembered what Mutther had told me about paving the way for others like me. The Hotel fountain had no representation for my kind, and I had to wonder how many half-breeds like me existed —hiding in plain sight, trying not to be noticed or worse, thinking they weren't good enough.

"Sorry," I said to Holden, "I can't let this happen. I want justice for Myra, and I want justice for you.

This is wrong. Leon is wrong."

Silas smiled encouragingly, and I realized he wanted Holden to be innocent. He wanted me to prove Leon wrong, and maybe the real reason I'd been sent to the Hotel wasn't to bring Holden back to be punished for Myra's death, but to bring him home where he belonged to face what it meant to be a clan leader.

I swallowed the lump of fear stuck in my throat, walked determinedly to the fire pit, and stood beside Holden. "I declare the right to be a primary character witness for the defense."

The collective intake of breath made a whooshing sound, followed by a hum of excitement. I caught a few nods of approval, but just as many groused at my declaration. I stood tall to face my naysayers. "My name is Janda Gray. I'm a bounty hunter hired by Silas to lure Alexander Holden out from his safe haven."

The grumblings intensified. I ventured a glance at Holden and wished I hadn't. The pain of betrayal had turned his brilliant golden eyes a dark umber, and I had to force myself to continue. "I've read the same facts presented to you this evening, and like many of you, I was convinced of Holden's complicity." I stared at Leon until he couldn't meet my gaze any longer and turned to speak to his neighbor. "Then I met him in his panther form as he hunted for food—not a smart move on my part. He had me cornered. I ran, and by all rights he could have killed me." I started at one end of the semicircle and met the gazes of each person all the way to the opposite side. "He didn't hurt me. He was in animal form at the height of a hunt, and he didn't harm me in any way."

Leon stepped out from the line of his followers. "That just shows what I'm saying about him being cold and calculating. He can control his inner panther. Myra's death was planned. You didn't prove me wrong. You proved me right."

He twisted my words until the crowd's discontent rang out once more. I glanced at Silas, but he shook his head. Nick gave me a nod to keep going. This was my game. I had to play my hand and hope I'd win the clan over.

"Holden didn't have to leave his safety to come back here. He was concerned about his clan, about Silas, and about you, Leon." I glared at him. "Which is more than I can say for you." I turned in a circle, scanning the crowd. "A true leader does what is best for his people. Holden left so your loyalties wouldn't be divided. He left to keep his clan intact." My voice rose higher, carried on the fall breeze above the flames and out over the trees.

Leon glowered at me and stepped closer. "He didn't want to be our leader. My sister's death was the only way he could get out of it. He ran off—a coward afraid to face what he'd done."

Holden lowered his head, and his shoulders drooped. I couldn't let him take that blame. If the Hotel had done anything, it had shown me Holden's true nature—a leader—even if Holden didn't recognize it himself. This was the man who had taught me about love—how to love someone else and how I could finally love myself.

"He's here now. He's ready to sacrifice himself to

save his people. He thought a rival group might be attempting a takeover, so he sent me back to warn you. Before I could do that, Asher crossed my path. He and I have a long history. He attacked me, and if it hadn't been for Holden, I'd probably be dead. And you still think those are the actions of a killer?" I turned to the crowd. "You should be ashamed of yourselves. Look at what he's done for you, and look at how you've treated him."

I didn't think I could add anything else—except the truth about me.

"I'm not much for politics, and Holden sure as hell would prefer not to get mired in it, but he's a good man. He doesn't judge people for what they are, but for who they are inside. I know this firsthand. I'm a Lykoi."

The word half-breed surrounded me, scorching me more than if the flames from the pit caught me on fire. I held my head high and continued to blaze my path—to victory or hell, I'd soon find out.

"He's seen my true nature and accepted me as I am—as an equal." I couldn't look at Holden. If I did, I'd never get through this.

"My father was a new werecat who dared to love a beautiful wolf. For that, he was ostracized and badgered until he couldn't take it any longer. He killed himself to spare me and my mother. She died of grief shortly after I was born, and I was raised by her pack. Asher tormented me my whole life. He had no love for werecat women, and it's my belief he killed Myra because of what she was." I'd learned about my parents from the hushed whispers that filtered through my pack, usually when I'd done something that ended with me being reprimanded by Uncle. My mixed breed had been considered unstable, unnatural. I'd never faced my heritage head-on. It was long overdue.

I walked calmly over to Silas. "I don't want your bounty money. You know in your heart I'm right about Holden, so do something about it."

Regret was evident on Silas's face, and I understood he couldn't step in. The clan must decide. This was clan justice. One person didn't rule them, only guided them. Silas was a good leader and had done all he could. So had I.

"You've heard both sides," he said. "Now it's time to cast your vote."

I hadn't noticed the bronze bowl near the fire. It held what appeared to be stones — white and black. The first person stepped forward, withdrew a white one and tossed it into the flames. White smoke billowed forth.

"Innocent," he said, walking to the opposite side of the pit.

Leon snatched a black stone that overpowered the white smoke with black when he threw it into the fire. "Guilty."

He took a spot across from the first person who had voted. One by one the people cast their votes and lined up according to the color they'd chosen. All chatter had stopped, the only words spoken were that of the votes cast. I held my breath until my chest hurt and I had to force myself to breathe normally. This was awful. The lines were fairly even — a division among the clan and exactly what Holden had tried to avoid.

Three people remained, not counting Silas, who I assumed wasn't allowed to vote. Nick made no motion to join in, and when I would have cast my vote, Silas simply put out his hand and held mine. We could only wait for the final decision.

A flash of light blurred my vision. At first I thought a stone had exploded into a brilliance of white then I saw Sebastian.

I half expected the clan to attack, but no one moved. Sebastian glided towards us, past Holden without giving him the slightest notice, to stop in front of Silas.

"Greetings, old friend. Pardon the interruption. We have come to lend our aid." Sebastian seemed to have fully recovered from whatever had ailed him. His skin was no longer a pasty yellow, but a luminescent white that was almost ghost-like. I was quite impressed. Of course, I was also pretty sure that was the effect he was after — very theatrical.

Silas gave Sebastian a wary look and glanced beyond him. I followed his gaze. A group of men and women had taken position at the edge of the clearing, where the firelight met darkness to blanket the newcomers in shadows. Mutther came forward, and with him came Uncle.

"Niece," Uncle said.

"Uncle Damon."

I barely managed the response, but he didn't seem to think more was needed. He nodded to me, then joined the walking dead man. I raised my brows at Mutther, who quirked a smile and took his place near Silas.

"My apologies," Mutther said, "but I felt it my

duty to come straight here after learning some very disturbing news."

"Oh," Silas said. "And the others thought it necessary to come as well? This is highly irregular. A man's fate is being decided, and you bring guests?"

"I wouldn't have come if it wasn't important. I'll let Sebastian explain. He's the horse's mouth."

I hid my laugh with a polite fake sneeze.

"Bless you," Uncle said.

"Thanks," I replied, doing my best not to smile.

"Really. I'm hardly a horse's mouth, or any other part of one, if you don't mind." Sebastian's indignant tone had even Uncle covering his mouth to hide a smile.

"Please get on with it," Silas said.

"Quite," Sebastian said, still ruffled. "If you would allow me a moment, I'll tell you about our meeting this evening."

"Of course."

The meeting in question was the big to-do that Mutther had mentioned. I was anxious to hear what it had to do with Holden's trial.

"Mutther filled us in on your current situation and how the outcome might affect our group dynamics. We pursued his line of questioning regarding territorial issues and discovered something amiss. We felt it prudent to address it immediately, which brings us here at the present moment."

The clan lines that had formed during the voting disintegrated into a cluster of people gathering around to hear what Sebastian had to say. Holden had been left unattended, so I eased my way over to him. He held my hand, his chains clanking lightly. I could have cried at his gesture of acceptance. If we survived this night, we'd have a great deal to discuss, but at least he hadn't turned away from me. That was a start.

Sebastian's voice reached us loud and clear. He spoke for all to hear, even though he addressed Silas. "A rumor has spread that your territory is up for grabs."

Silas clenched his fists. "That's not true."

"Of course not," Sebastian said. "I did say it was a rumor, not fact. Rumors can be a problem, however, so we wanted to nip that one fast. We've been unable to pinpoint its origin other than it started within your clan."

"That's absurd. Why would one of my clan folk say such a thing?"

"Our thoughts precisely. So we dug deeper and found Asher at the center, along with a picture I believe you have in your possession." Sebastian's speech sped up, his excitement coming out in his voice. "And that's not all we found." At this point Sebastian shoved Uncle Damon into the middle of their little group discussion. "Damon will take it from here."

Damon Gray was the complete opposite of Sebastian. His stern demeanor was familiar to me, and I recognized he was holding his anger at bay.

"I offer my condolences for your loss," he said, referring to Myra. "It must be a terrible shock for you to lose the sunshine of your life, especially on the heels of the loss of your wife and your second in such a tragic car crash. I know how I would feel if something were to happen to my Janda."

I froze in total shock. Uncle never talked about emotions. He never even said he loved me. Holden gripped my hand tighter, and I realized I was shaking. I knew Uncle had loved my mother. She was his little sister, and I always thought it was out of respect for her that he hadn't sent me away. I was wrong. He really did care about me.

"Thank you," Silas said. "Please continue."

"It's difficult to admit when I've failed, which makes coming here tonight doubly painful. I hope that you'll hear me out and perhaps find it in you to forgive an old fool."

"We're all old fools, but I don't understand what you're getting at."

"Asher was an angry man. His anger turned him into something ugly, something I had turned a blind eye to, hoping he'd come around to accepting Janda." He sighed. "He didn't, and when I gave him an ultimatum to either put aside his prejudice or leave, he took off."

"And you think that's why he killed Myra?" Sadness filled Silas's words. "It's not your fault. None of us can say for sure what someone will do when their soul's been poisoned like his."

Sebastian handed something to Uncle, but I couldn't tell what it was. Uncle passed it to Silas. A faint glow of backlight filled his palm—a phone.

"Sebastian contacted me after Janda left the Hotel. He was concerned for her safety. Once Asher was killed, I thought everything would settle down. I didn't count on my stubborn niece falling in love with Holden."

Uncle turned to me, and all I could do was shrug.

"I had no choice but to help Sebastian clear Holden. I want my niece happy, and keeping Holden alive is the only way I can make that happen. And I also don't want to see an innocent man condemned."

Leon strode to the center of the gathering. "This is all warm and fuzzy, but it doesn't change the fact that Holden murdered my sister. I demand the trial continue."

Silas scrolled through the phone, ignoring his nephew's outburst. "The trial is over," he said. He removed a key from a rope around his neck and handed it to Mutther. "Release Holden."

Mutther unlocked the padlocks and ripped the chains off Holden, helping him to his feet and patting him on the back.

"What just happened?" I was stunned.

"Proof that Holden is innocent," Mutther said, grinning and still thumping Holden's back.

Leon backed away from us. Silas advanced on him and threw the phone into the dirt at Leon's feet.

"Asher's phone with the picture on it that you presented as belonging to an anonymous bystander who wanted the truth to be told." Silas stood a foot away from his nephew. "You took this picture."

"No. I told you it came in an unmarked envelope."

"Don't lie. You doctored the image—superimposed Holden into the picture. Asher's text messages tell what really happened." He shook his head. "How could you have your own sister killed?"

Leon dropped his act, lunging at his uncle. Silas landed a blow that sent Leon reeling backward.

"Take him," Silas said, "before I tear him apart."

"You've grown weak and stupid," Leon said, his features twisting in his rage. "I'm glad you lost your mate, although the car accident was supposed to only have killed your second." Spit flew from Leon as his anger escalated. "I should have been his replacement! You chose Holden over your own flesh and blood! You had to be stopped! The car crash wasn't enough. You're the reason my sister had to be sacrificed. Her blood is on your hands."

Silas stared dully at his nephew, as if he'd used up all his emotions. "Leon Vang you are hereby exiled from our clan, and as such will be turned over to the human authorities for prosecution unless Holden chooses to end this by challenging you to combat. May God have mercy on your soul."

He walked away from his thrashing nephew, picked up a black stone from the bronze bowl and threw it into the fire. A giant plume of dark smoke rose from the flames.

"Guilty," he said. "Your fate is now in Holden's hands."

Holden's jaw muscles clenched. His posture taut, his gaze furious, he snatched a black stone and let the fire consume it. Holden spoke through the heavy, dark smoke circling Leon.

"Get him out of here."

EPILOGUE

The business card warmed my jacket pocket. I pulled it out. The front was the same with the words *the Hotel* printed in bold letters. I turned it over to find the other side was still blank.

"What's that supposed to mean?" I said, handing it to Holden.

"You never know with the Hotel." He put it on the nightstand and tossed another pair of jeans into a suitcase.

We were packing for a much needed vacation and the opportunity to finally get some alone time to explore our relationship. The preview he'd given me the night before of what we'd be doing on our trip left me exhausted but exceedingly happy. That man had stamina, and we'd found our biological differences weren't an issue. We mated in human form and shifted to hunt in designated areas in the woods of Sleepy Hollow — Lykoi and panther running together, tasting the freedom of being alive.

Holden had spent the two days following Leon's arrest sorting out clan business, including the particulars of Leon ending up in a top-secret division within the human justice system that dealt with paranormal criminals like Leon. I was now privy to a side of my world I hadn't known existed—outside of rumors—but it was family matters that concerned me more. Uncle Damon and I spent long hours talking, and our heart-to-heart had gone far better than I'd expected. Old wounds would take time to heal, but we were speaking openly about my mother and father and about my love for Holden. I received Uncle's blessing, although he still worried I'd get hurt and threatened to skin Holden alive if he ever mistreated me. Holden thought Uncle was kidding. He wasn't.

Sebastian's mark still remained, much to my annoyance. Turned out he was head of the Council of Elders who were responsible for maintaining the balance of power in the territories around Sleepy Hollow. The Elders wanted to recruit me to track down other paranormals who threatened the area. Leon was nothing. Worse creatures roamed these parts, giving new life to old legends and stirring up trouble for the inhabitants. I found out a hidden prison for highly dangerous supernaturals existed in Sleepy Hollow—had for centuries—and as with any prison, there were escapes. Stories arose to account for such episodes. Many became the origins for tales such as those Irving penned so long ago. Who knew the Headless Horseman was real? I never did.

I had a lot to think about. Taking on an official Hunter role was a big responsibility and would impact my life with Holden—just one more thing he and I had to work through. I felt bad for him. Not only did he have to face Uncle Damon, he had Silas to deal with as well. Silas had changed his mind about giving up his position as head of the clan, which pleased Holden to no end, until Silas told him the clan had held another voting session. They'd decided unanimously to make Holden their next leader, which was to take effect once Silas stepped down. The date had yet to be negotiated.

It seemed like a good idea to get out of town as soon as possible. We didn't have any plans on where we'd go, just to hop on our Harleys and ride.

"Aren't you done yet?" I couldn't believe a guy could take so long to pack a few clothes.

"Unlike you, I don't wear my outfits for several days in a row. It's called hygiene for a reason."

"Do I smell? No." I picked up my small duffle and headed out the door to load up Miss Kitty, snapping up the business card as I went by and jamming it back into my pocket. I tied down my bag and inspected her like I always did before going on a long drive then gave her a pat—truly a girl's best friend.

"Ready?" Holden said.

He pulled me to him and kissed me until my legs were like wet noodles—loose and rubbery. "Give me a minute."

He laughed and loaded up his bike. "You lead the way. I'll follow you anywhere you want to go."

"Anywhere?" I had a few places in mind. None of which required the clothes he'd packed.

"Why, Miss Gray, are you teasing me?"

"Not at all. I'm quite serious, Mr. Holden."

I had one leg over Miss Kitty when the card started to get super hot. I glanced at Holden, afraid one or the other of us was about to disappear. I didn't have a lot of faith in the Hotel's decision-making process.

"What's wrong?"

"The card," I said. "It's practically burning a hole in my pocket. What do I do?" I got off my bike and patted my jacket repeatedly—like that was going to help. "Ouch, damn it."

Holden tried helping me, but our fingers got tangled together in our effort to get to the card. He backed off so I could reach it.

"Take it out," he said. "Toss it. Why'd you pick it up anyway?"

"I don't know. It seemed irresponsible to leave it lying about." I yanked it free and was about to throw it on the ground when an address started to emerge and the card cooled off—The Woods, Sleepy Hollow.

We glanced at each other then at the woods in front of us.

"It can't be serious." I didn't see anything that looked like a portal in our vicinity.

We held hands and started walked closer to a tree I could swear hadn't been there before. "Do you think, you know, maybe. . ."

As soon as we got within a few feet of the massive oak, its leaves began to shimmer. We stepped closer, still holding hands.

"Don't you let go," I said.

"Never," he replied, tightening his grip.

The light blinded me, just as it had when I passed through it at Mutther's bar. I slipped beneath an archway of bark and ended up in a tropical forest. We were back in Holden's jungle inside the Hotel's Green Room. He was by my side, our fingers intertwined. He'd never let go, and in that moment I knew he'd always be there for me, as I would be for him.

The splash of water hitting rocks grew louder as we pushed past vines and heavy scented flowers. The waterfall was just as I'd remembered—or almost anyway.

Behind the curtain of water, something shiny caught a ray of light and glinted out at us. We stepped over a pathway of boulders that took us into a cave I hadn't seen the last time we were here. I started laughing at what had been reflecting the light. The Hotel must have sensed what I'd meant about Holden following me anywhere.

"The Hotel does provide for its guests," he said, taking me to a large brass bed.

"It certainly does."

I stripped and began helping him do the same. This was going to be an amazing vacation, especially since here, in this dimension, we'd have plenty of time to spend together.

ABOUT THE AUTHOR

Sheri Queen received her MFA in Writing Popular Fiction from Seton Hill University. She grew up in the Hudson Valley region of New York—an area she loves to depict as a backdrop for her stories—and enjoys traveling to new places where she is constantly discovering inspirations for her writing.

Follow Sheri online and sign up for notifications: www.sheriqueen.com

Made in the USA
San Bernardino, CA
30 August 2017